BEYOND™

VOLUME 10:
CURSED!

Written by
R.L. Stine

Illustrated by
Kelly & Nichole Matthews

Lettered by
Mike Fiorentino

Cover by
Miguel Mercado

Just Beyond created by
R.L. Stine

Designer
Scott Newman

Associate Editor
Sophie Philips-Roberts

Editor
Bryce Carlson

 Spotlight

ABDOBOOKS.COM

Reinforced library bound edition published in 2022 by Spotlight, a division of ABDO, PO Box 398166, Minneapolis, Minnesota 55439. Spotlight produces high-quality reinforced library bound editions for schools and libraries.
Published by agreement with KaBOOM!

Printed in the United States of America, North Mankato, Minnesota.
042021
092021

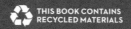

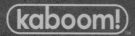

THIS BOOK CONTAINS RECYCLED MATERIALS

kaboom!™

BOOM! Studios, 5670 Wilshire Boulevard, Suite 400, Los Angeles, CA 90036-5679.

Library of Congress Control Number: 2020947942

Publisher's Cataloging-in-Publication Data

Names: Stine, R.L., author. | Matthews, Kelly; Matthews, Nichole, illustrators.
Title: Cursed! / by R.L. Stine ; illustrated by Kelly Matthews and Nichole Matthews.
Description: Minneapolis, Minnesota : Spotlight, 2022. | Series: Just beyond; volume 10
Summary: Ramar brings a swamp beast named Koroko out of hiding to eat Karla, Benny, and Bill, but the Harlans escape into the woods where they meet a friend and try to figure out how to cure Benny's beastly bite.
Identifiers: ISBN 9781532148293 (lib. bdg.)
Subjects: LCSH: Brothers and sisters--Juvenile fiction. | Monsters--Juvenile fiction. | Healing--Juvenile fiction. | Ghost stories--Juvenile fiction. | Middle school students--Juvenile fiction. | Graphic novels--Juvenile fiction.
Classification: DDC 741.5--dc23

ABDO
Spotlight
A Division of ABDO
abdobooks.com

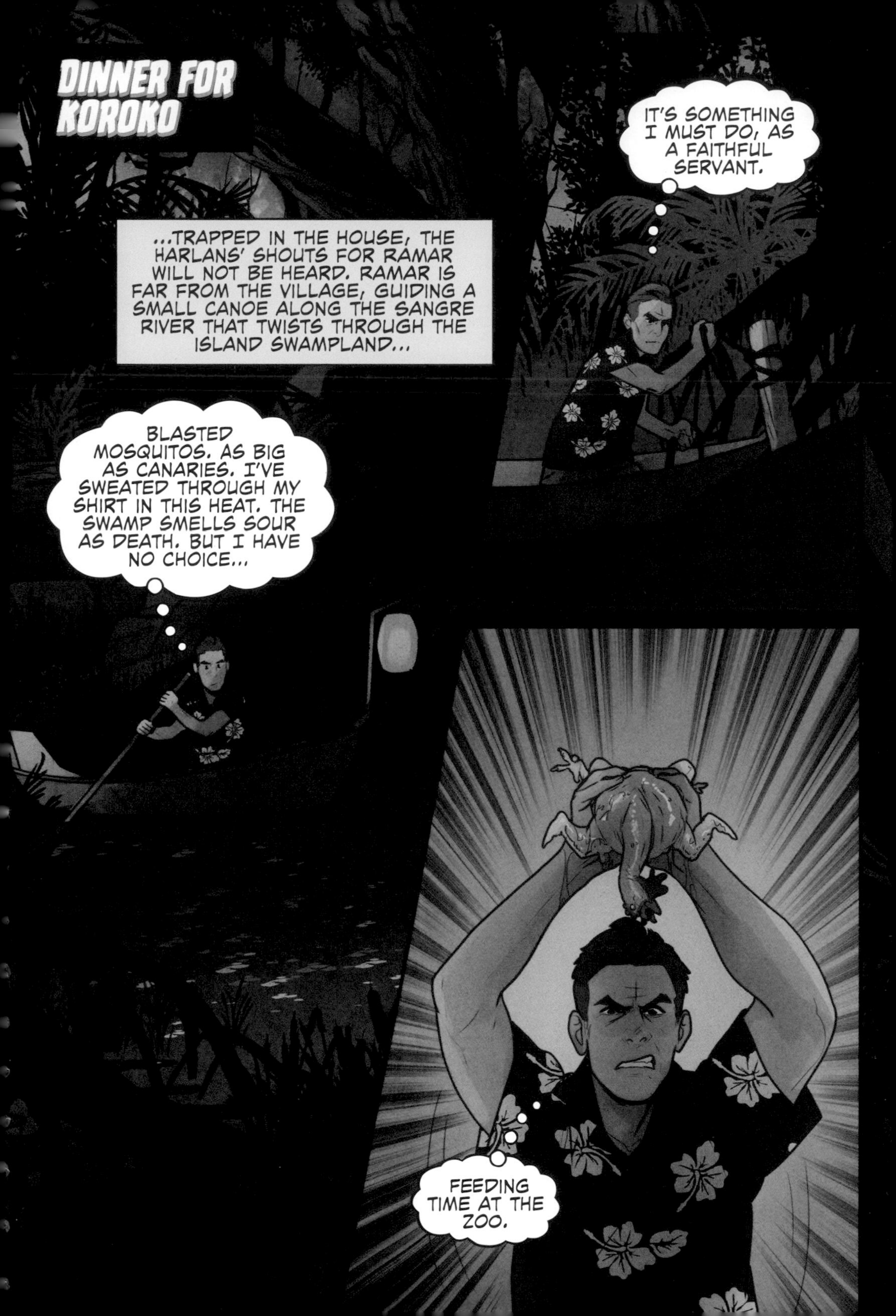
DINNER FOR KOROKO
...TRAPPED IN THE HOUSE, THE HARLANS' SHOUTS FOR RAMAR WILL NOT BE HEARD. RAMAR IS FAR FROM THE VILLAGE, GUIDING A SMALL CANOE ALONG THE SANGRE RIVER THAT TWISTS THROUGH THE ISLAND SWAMPLAND...
IT'S SOMETHING I MUST DO, AS A FAITHFUL SERVANT.
BLASTED MOSQUITOS. AS BIG AS CANARIES. I'VE SWEATED THROUGH MY SHIRT IN THIS HEAT. THE SWAMP SMELLS SOUR AS DEATH. BUT I HAVE NO CHOICE...
FEEDING TIME AT THE ZOO.

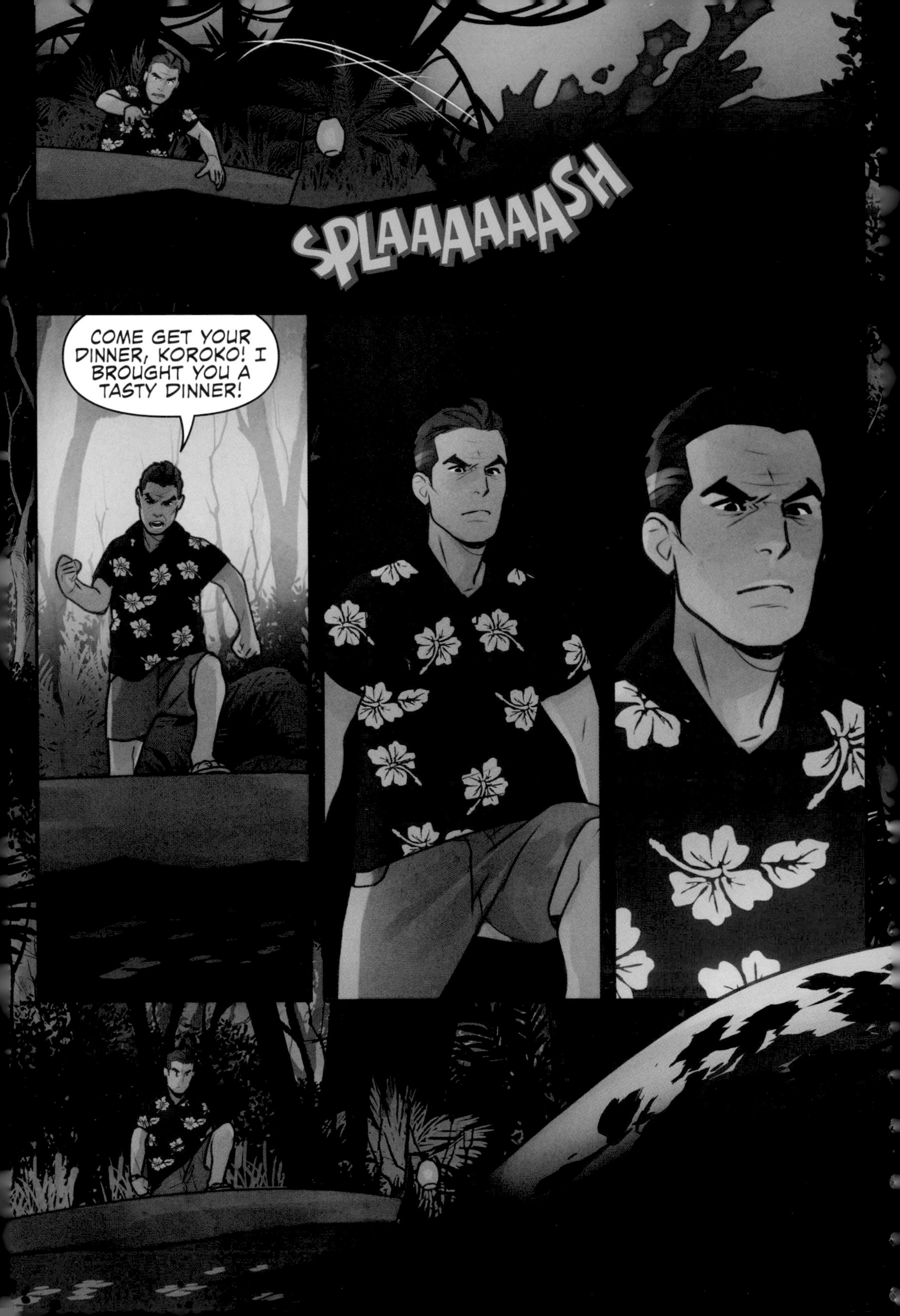
SPLAAAAAASH
COME GET YOUR DINNER, KOROKO! I BROUGHT YOU A TASTY DINNER!

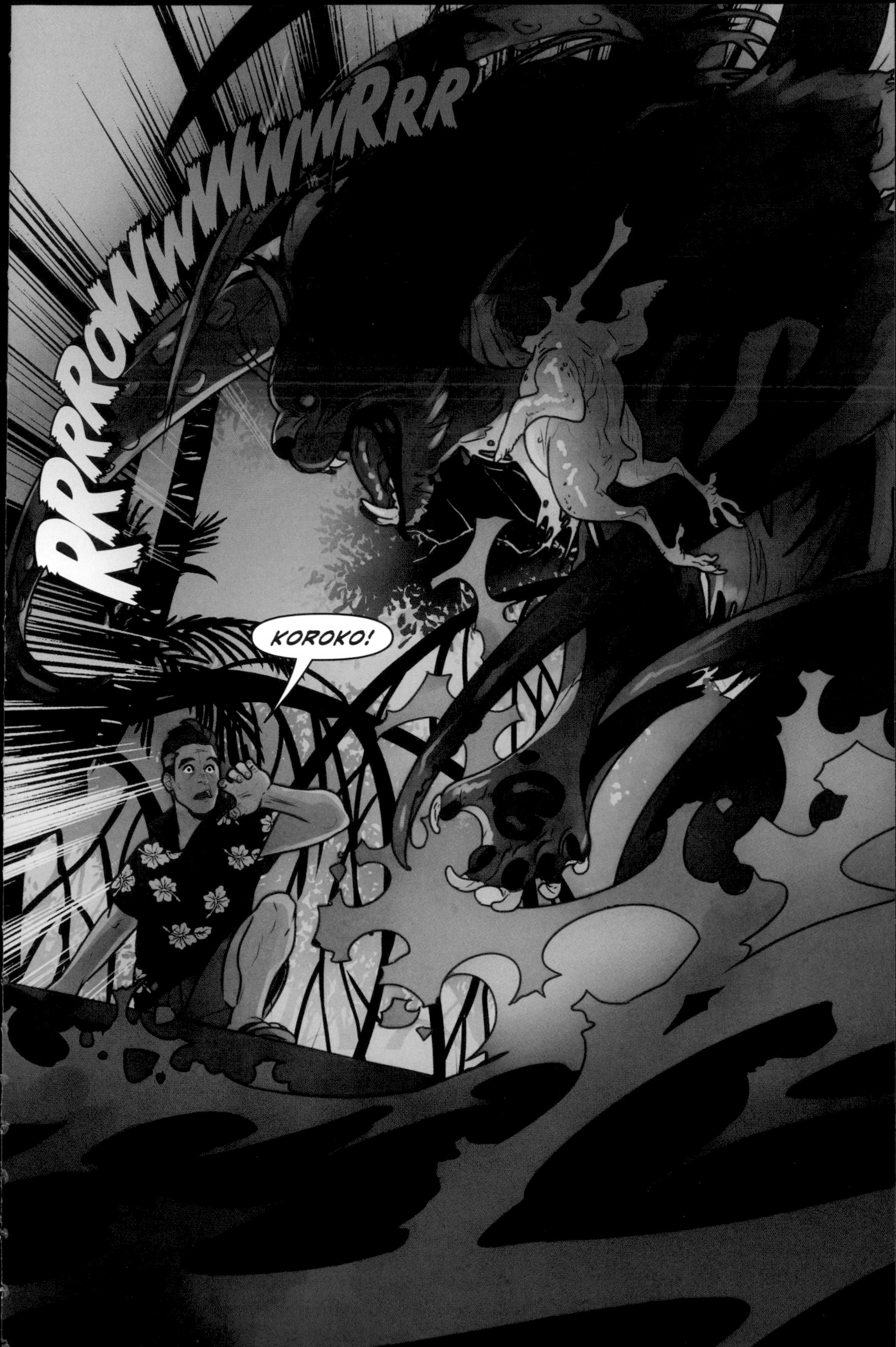

RRRROWWWWWWRRR
KOROKO!

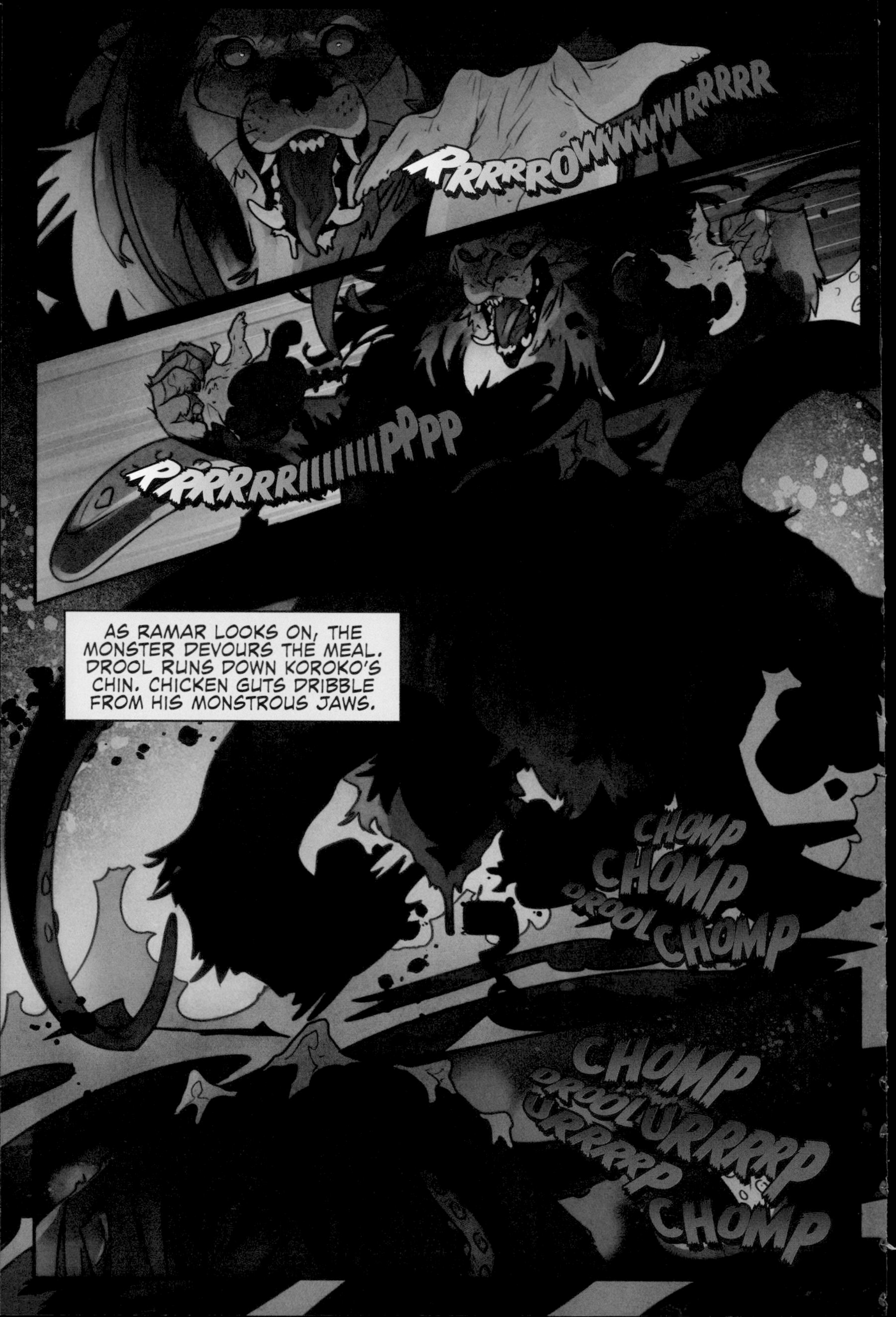
PRRRROWWWWWRRRRR
PRRRRRIIIIIIIIIPPPP
AS RAMAR LOOKS ON, THE MONSTER DEVOURS THE MEAL. DROOL RUNS DOWN KOROKO'S CHIN. CHICKEN GUTS DRIBBLE FROM HIS MONSTROUS JAWS.
CHOMP
CHOMP
DROOL
CHOMP
CHOMP
DROOL
URRRRRP
URRRRP
CHOMP

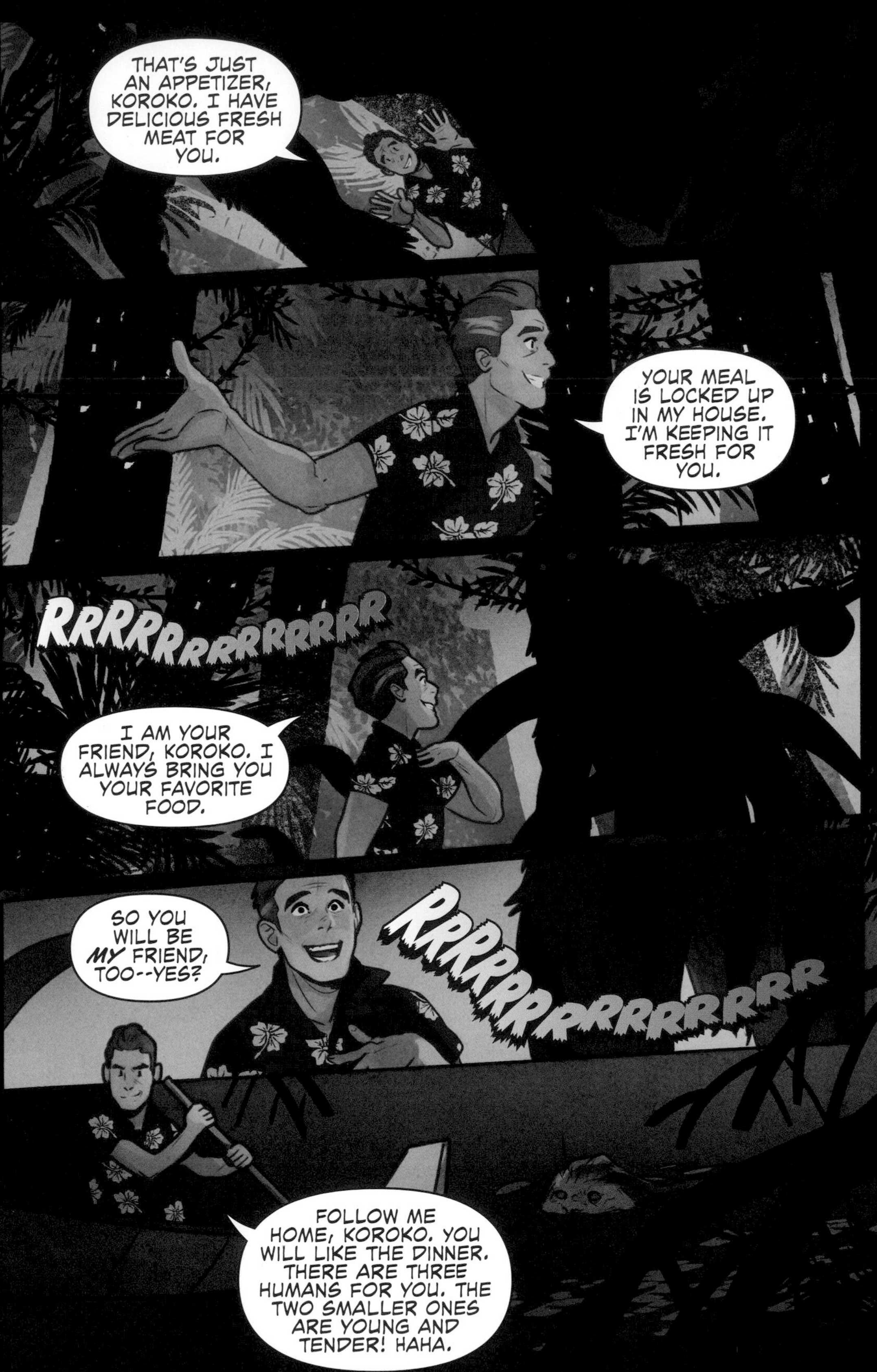
THAT'S JUST AN APPETIZER, KOROKO. I HAVE DELICIOUS FRESH MEAT FOR YOU.
YOUR MEAL IS LOCKED UP IN MY HOUSE. I'M KEEPING IT FRESH FOR YOU.
RRRRRRRRRRRRR
I AM YOUR FRIEND, KOROKO. I ALWAYS BRING YOU YOUR FAVORITE FOOD.
SO YOU WILL BE *MY* FRIEND, TOO--YES?
RRRRRRRRRRRRRRR
FOLLOW ME HOME, KOROKO. YOU WILL LIKE THE DINNER. THERE ARE THREE HUMANS FOR YOU. THE TWO SMALLER ONES ARE YOUNG AND TENDER! HAHA.

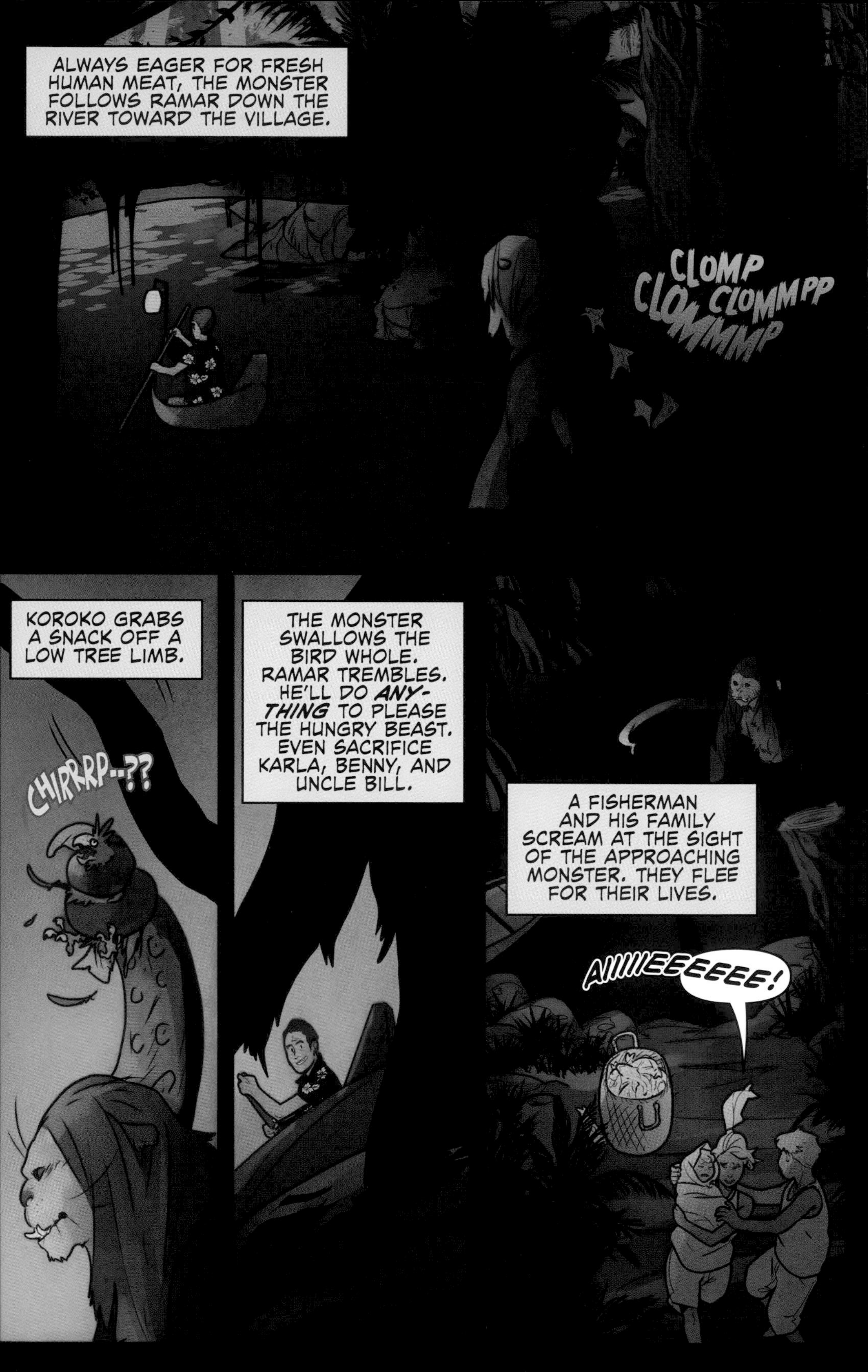
ALWAYS EAGER FOR FRESH HUMAN MEAT, THE MONSTER FOLLOWS RAMAR DOWN THE RIVER TOWARD THE VILLAGE.
CLOMP
CLOMMMP
CLOMMPP
KOROKO GRABS A SNACK OFF A LOW TREE LIMB.
CHIRRRP--??
THE MONSTER SWALLOWS THE BIRD WHOLE. RAMAR TREMBLES. HE'LL DO *ANY-THING* TO PLEASE THE HUNGRY BEAST. EVEN SACRIFICE KARLA, BENNY, AND UNCLE BILL.
A FISHERMAN AND HIS FAMILY SCREAM AT THE SIGHT OF THE APPROACHING MONSTER. THEY FLEE FOR THEIR LIVES.
AIIIIIEEEEEEE!

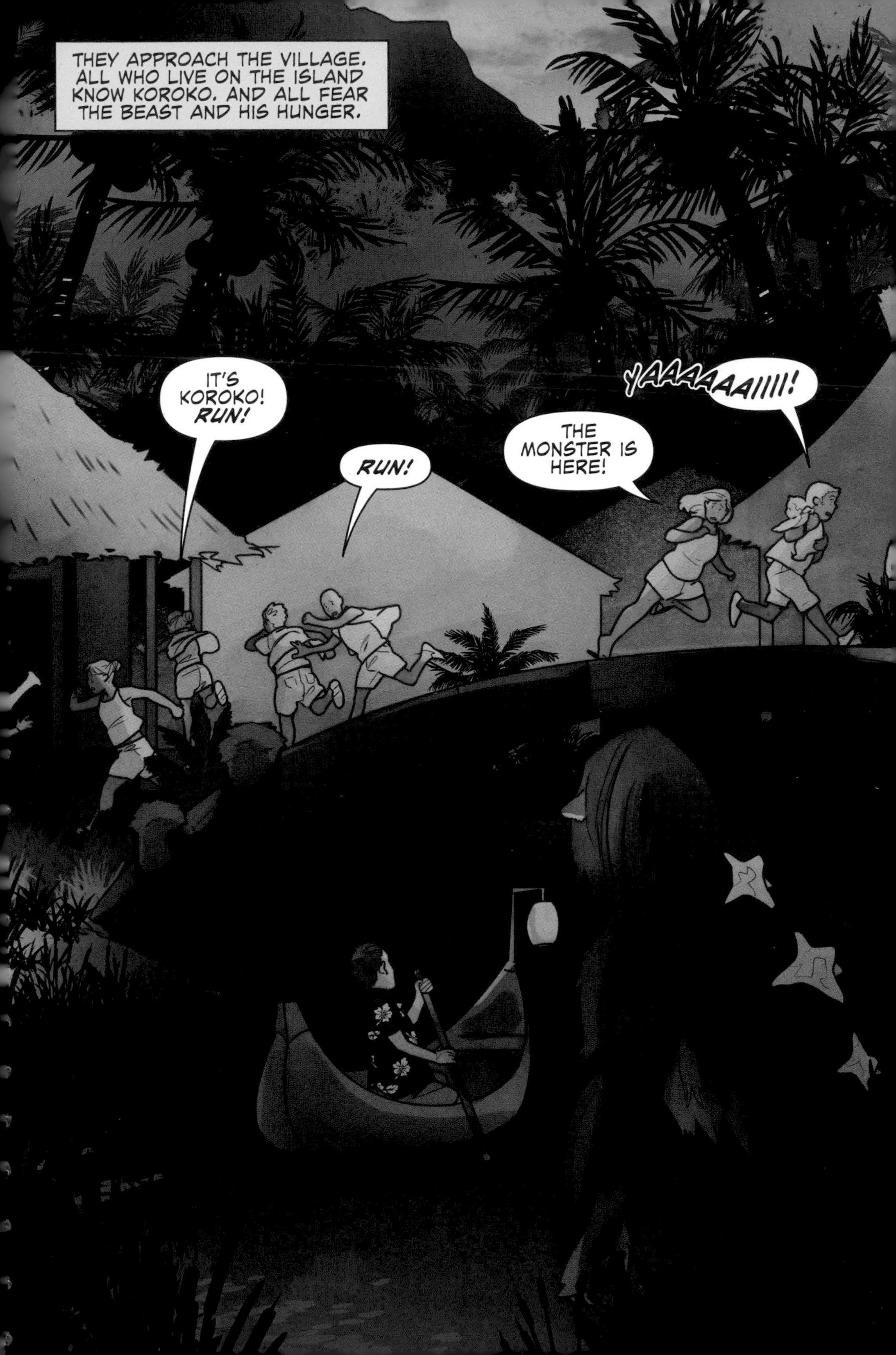
THEY APPROACH THE VILLAGE. ALL WHO LIVE ON THE ISLAND KNOW KOROKO. AND ALL FEAR THE BEAST AND HIS HUNGER.
IT'S KOROKO! *RUN!*
RUN!
YAAAAAAIIIII!
THE MONSTER IS HERE!

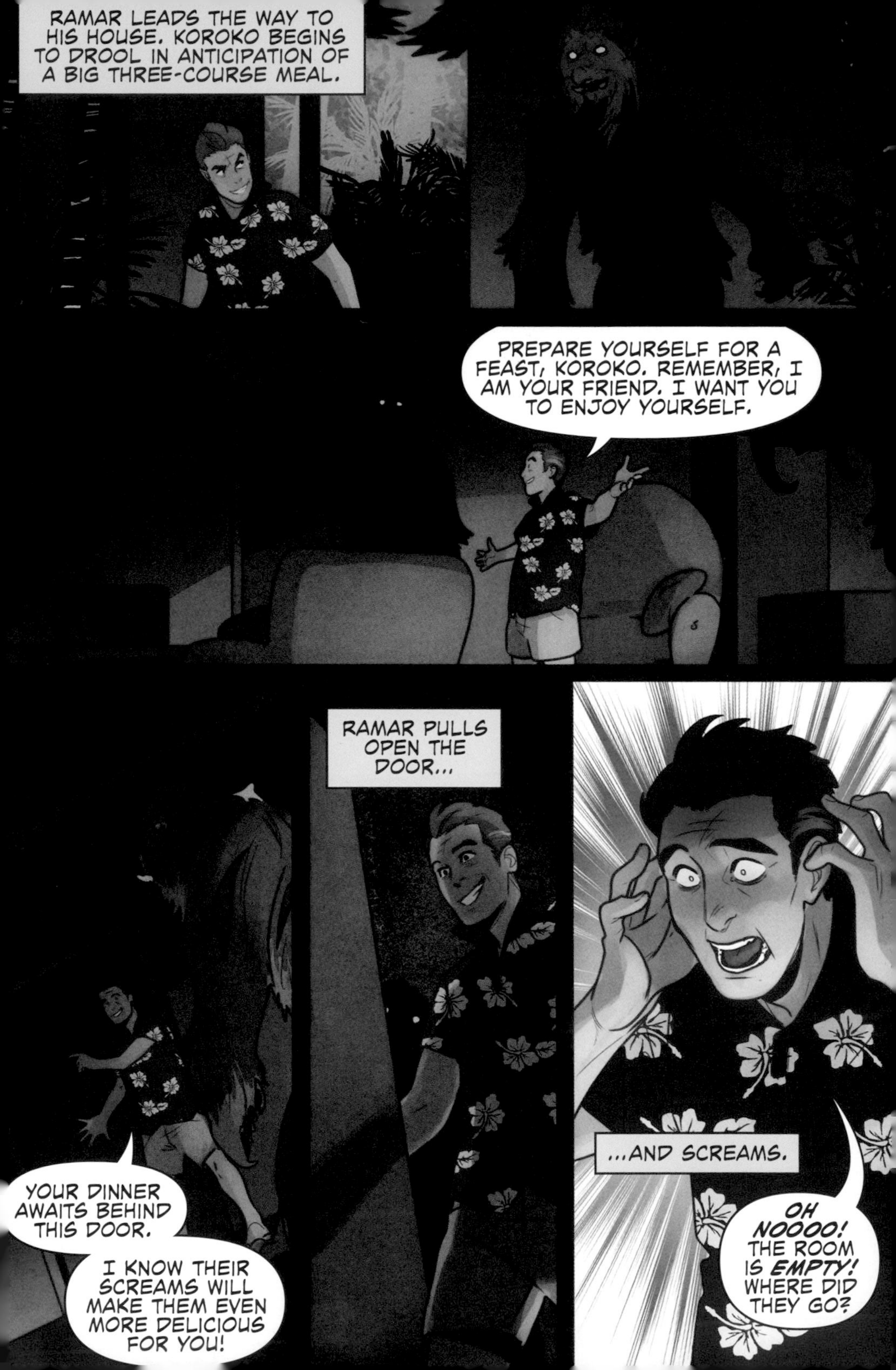
RAMAR LEADS THE WAY TO HIS HOUSE. KOROKO BEGINS TO DROOL IN ANTICIPATION OF A BIG THREE-COURSE MEAL.
PREPARE YOURSELF FOR A FEAST, KOROKO. REMEMBER, I AM YOUR FRIEND. I WANT YOU TO ENJOY YOURSELF.
YOUR DINNER AWAITS BEHIND THIS DOOR.
I KNOW THEIR SCREAMS WILL MAKE THEM EVEN MORE DELICIOUS FOR YOU!
RAMAR PULLS OPEN THE DOOR...
...AND SCREAMS.
OH NOOOO! THE ROOM IS EMPTY! WHERE DID THEY GO?

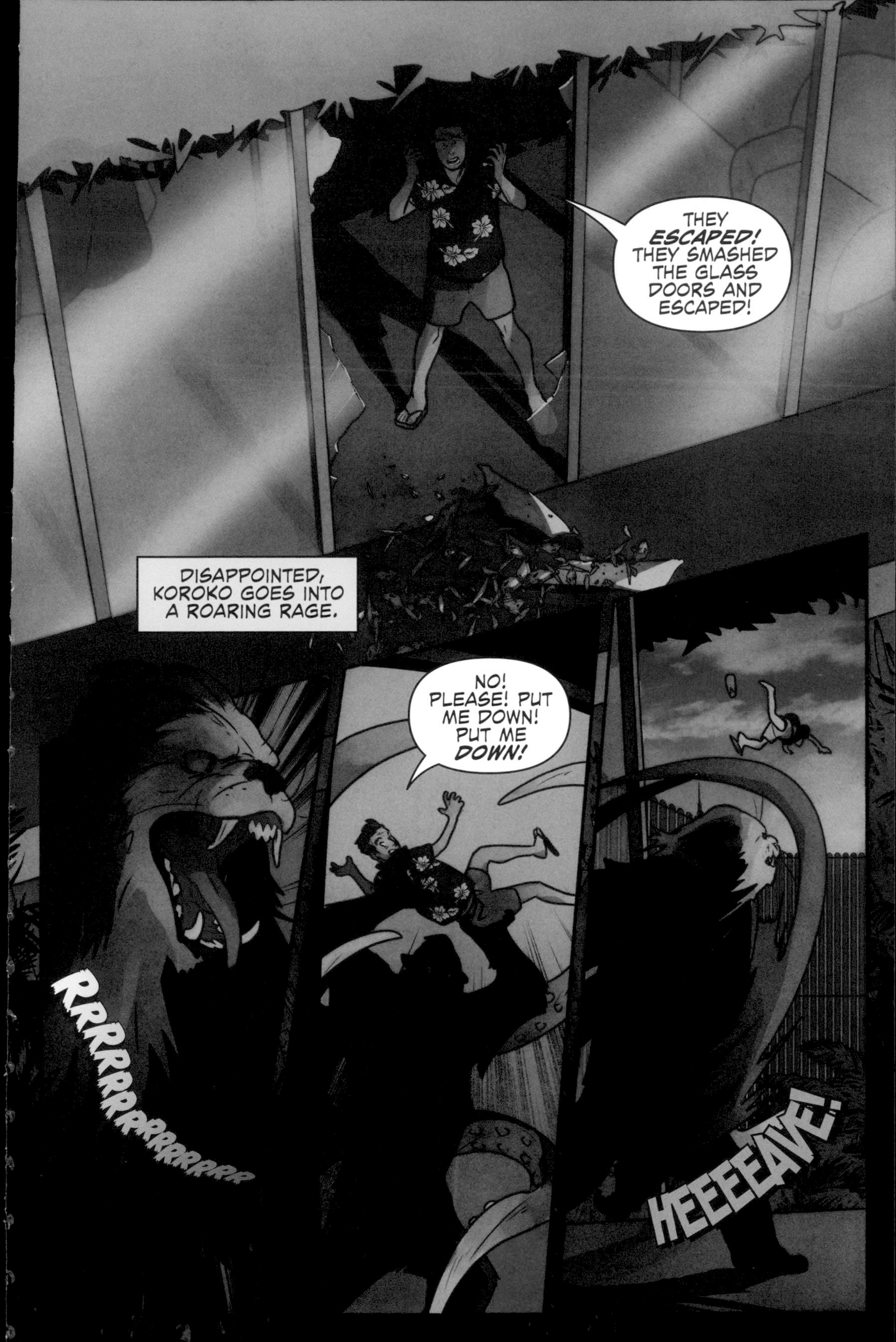
THEY ESCAPED! THEY SMASHED THE GLASS DOORS AND ESCAPED!
DISAPPOINTED, KOROKO GOES INTO A ROARING RAGE.
RRRRRRRRRRRRRRR
NO! PLEASE! PUT ME DOWN! PUT ME DOWN!
HEEEEAVE!

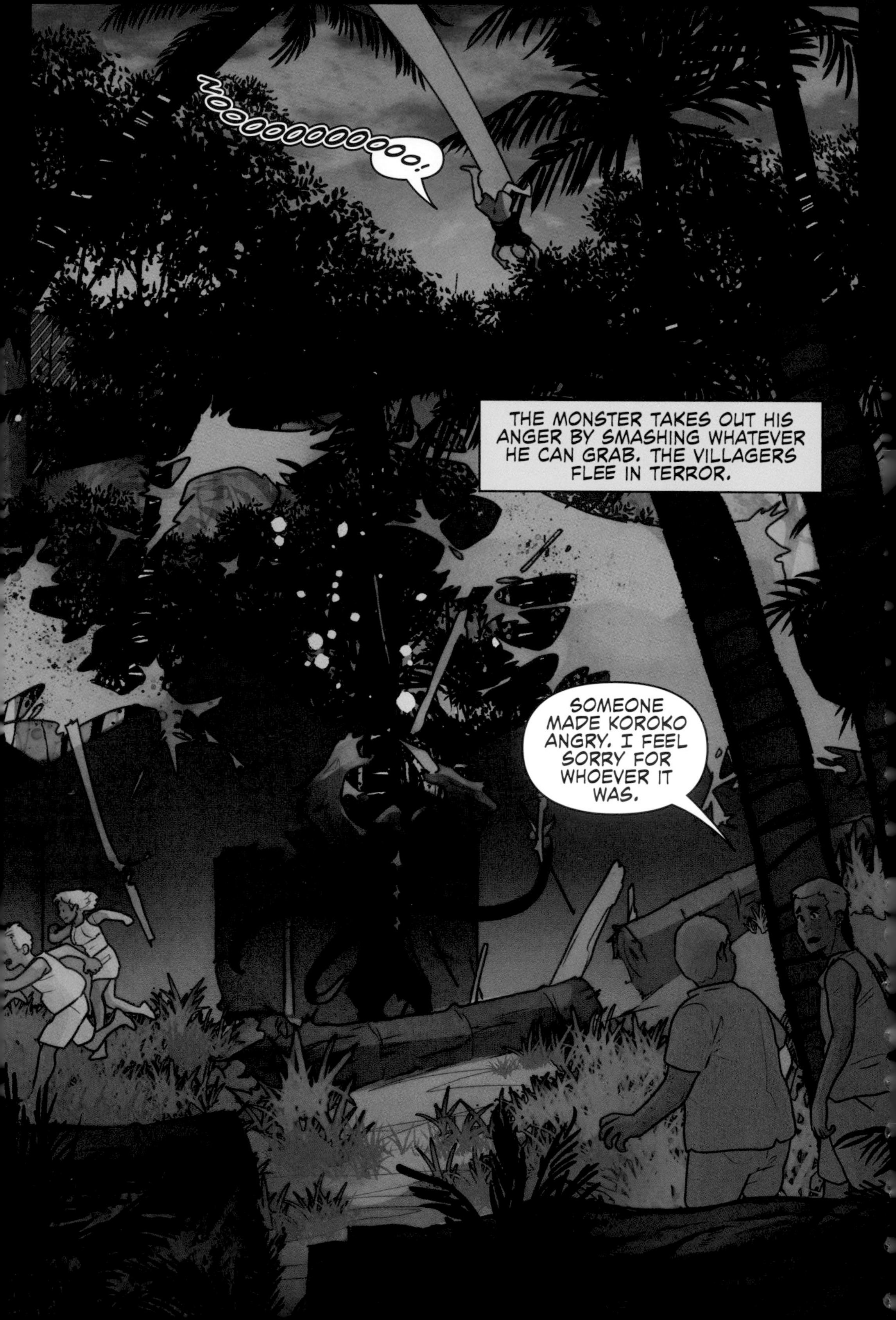
NOOOOOOOOOOOOO!
THE MONSTER TAKES OUT HIS ANGER BY SMASHING WHATEVER HE CAN GRAB. THE VILLAGERS FLEE IN TERROR.
SOMEONE MADE KOROKO ANGRY. I FEEL SORRY FOR WHOEVER IT WAS.

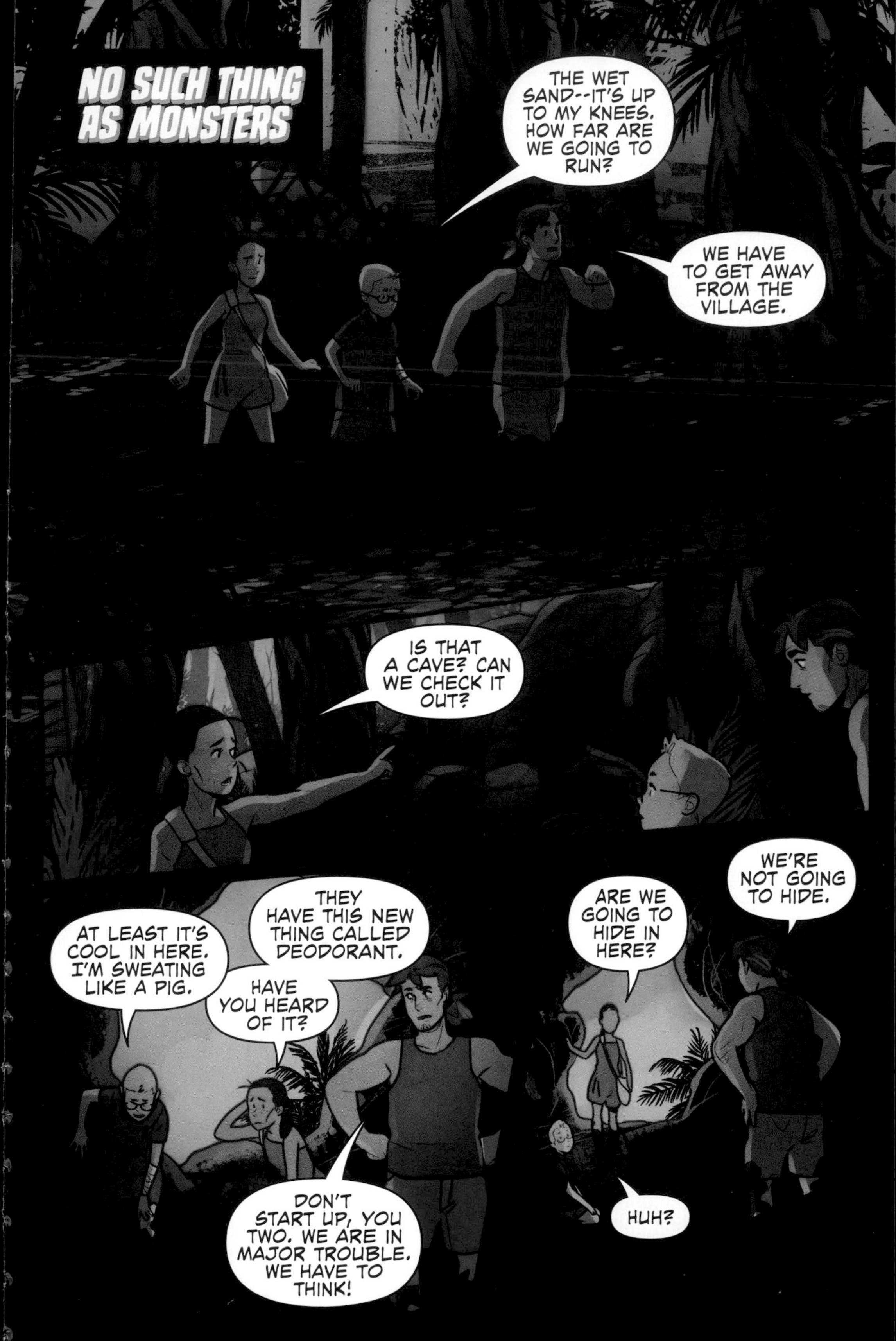
NO SUCH THING AS MONSTERS
THE WET SAND--IT'S UP TO MY KNEES. HOW FAR ARE WE GOING TO RUN?
WE HAVE TO GET AWAY FROM THE VILLAGE.
IS THAT A CAVE? CAN WE CHECK IT OUT?
AT LEAST IT'S COOL IN HERE. I'M SWEATING LIKE A PIG.
THEY HAVE THIS NEW THING CALLED DEODORANT.
HAVE YOU HEARD OF IT?
DON'T START UP, YOU TWO. WE ARE IN MAJOR TROUBLE. WE HAVE TO THINK!
ARE WE GOING TO HIDE IN HERE?
WE'RE NOT GOING TO HIDE.
HUH?

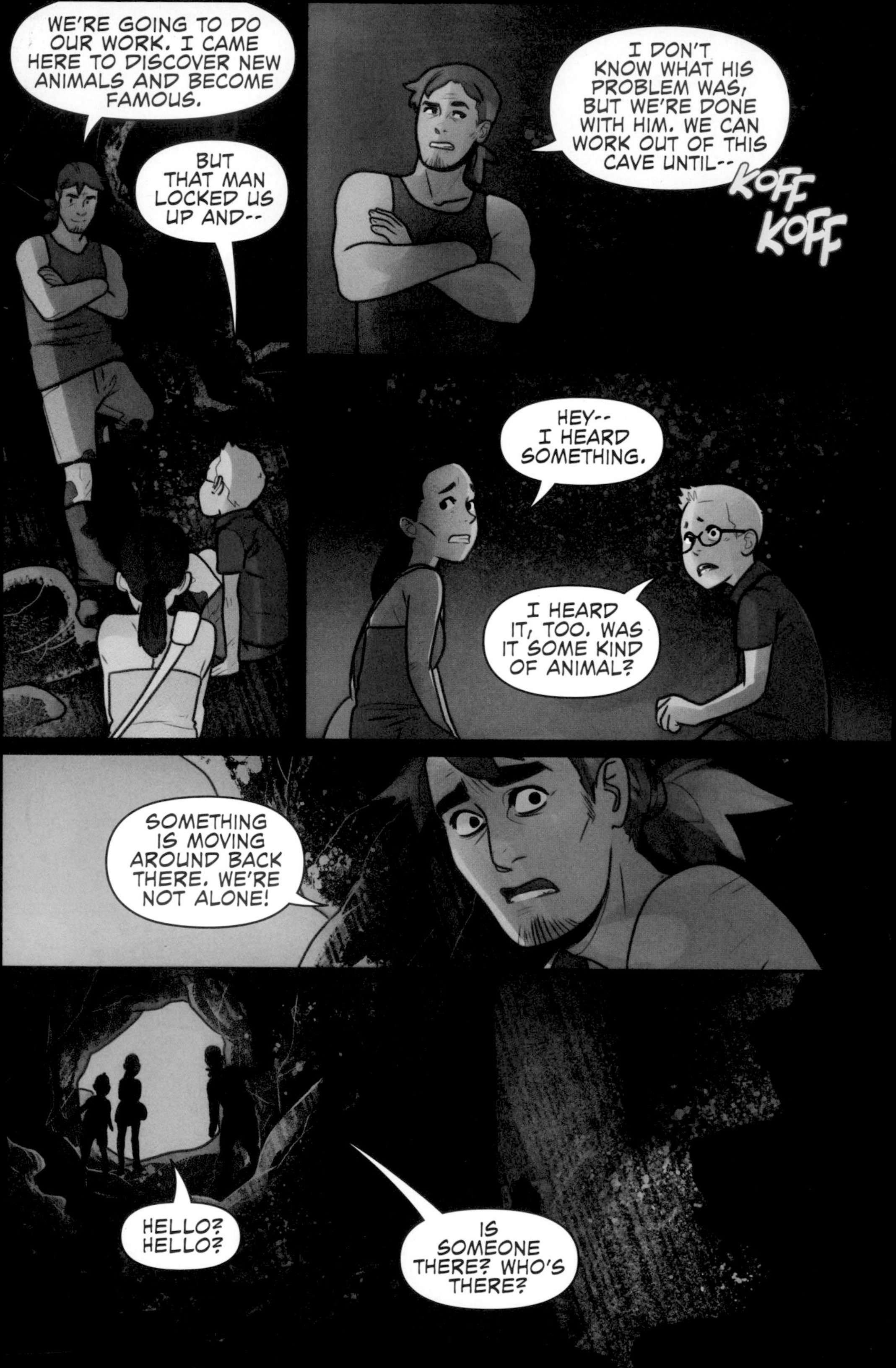
WE'RE GOING TO DO OUR WORK. I CAME HERE TO DISCOVER NEW ANIMALS AND BECOME FAMOUS.
BUT THAT MAN LOCKED US UP AND--
I DON'T KNOW WHAT HIS PROBLEM WAS, BUT WE'RE DONE WITH HIM. WE CAN WORK OUT OF THIS CAVE UNTIL--
KOFF KOFF
HEY-- I HEARD SOMETHING.
I HEARD IT, TOO. WAS IT SOME KIND OF ANIMAL?
SOMETHING IS MOVING AROUND BACK THERE. WE'RE NOT ALONE!
HELLO? HELLO?
IS SOMEONE THERE? WHO'S THERE?

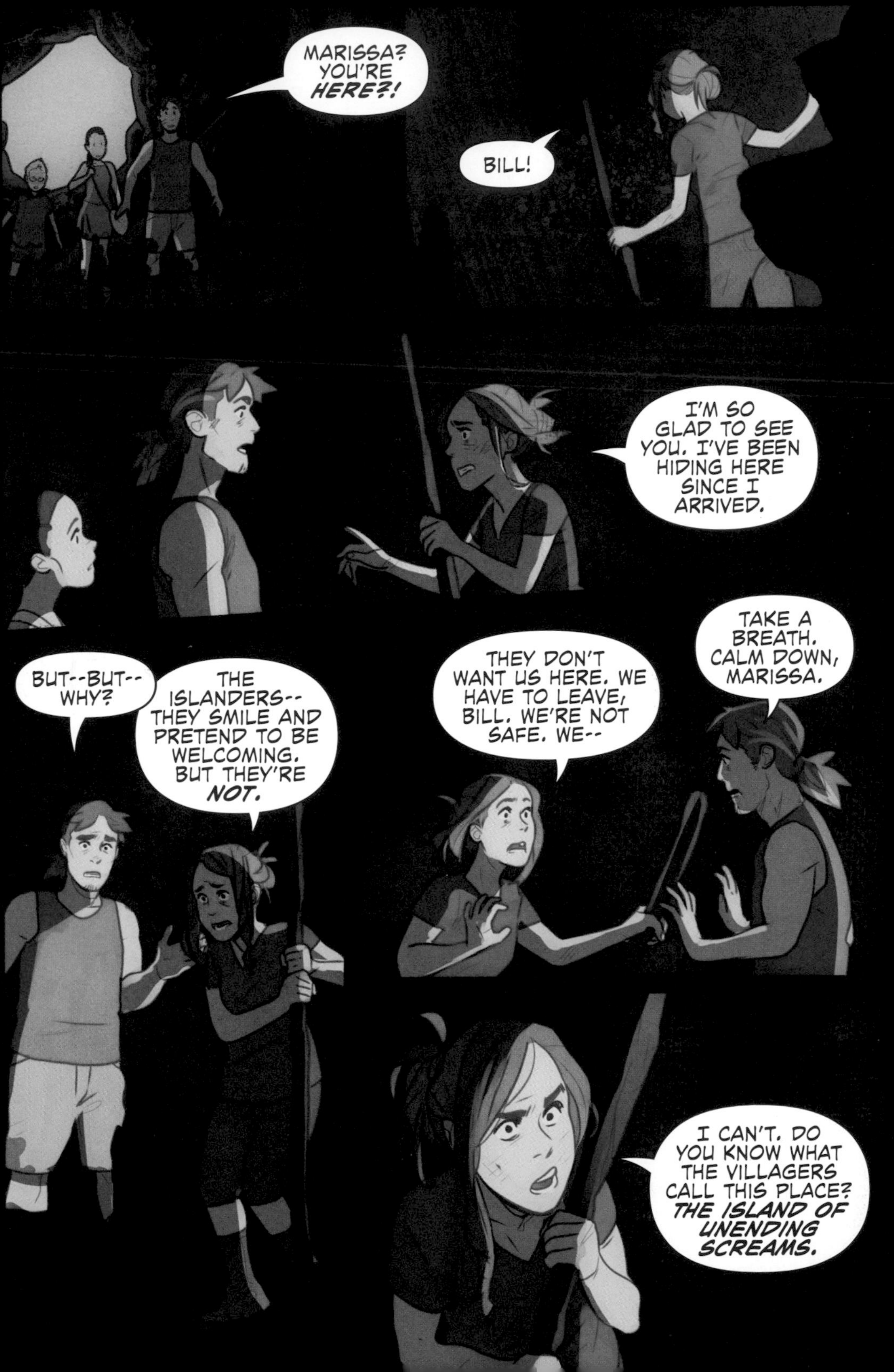
MARISSA? YOU'RE *HERE?!*
BILL!
I'M SO GLAD TO SEE YOU. I'VE BEEN HIDING HERE SINCE I ARRIVED.
BUT--BUT--WHY?
THE ISLANDERS--THEY SMILE AND PRETEND TO BE WELCOMING. BUT THEY'RE *NOT.*
THEY DON'T WANT US HERE. WE HAVE TO LEAVE, BILL. WE'RE NOT SAFE. WE--
TAKE A BREATH. CALM DOWN, MARISSA.
I CAN'T. DO YOU KNOW WHAT THE VILLAGERS CALL THIS PLACE? *THE ISLAND OF UNENDING SCREAMS.*

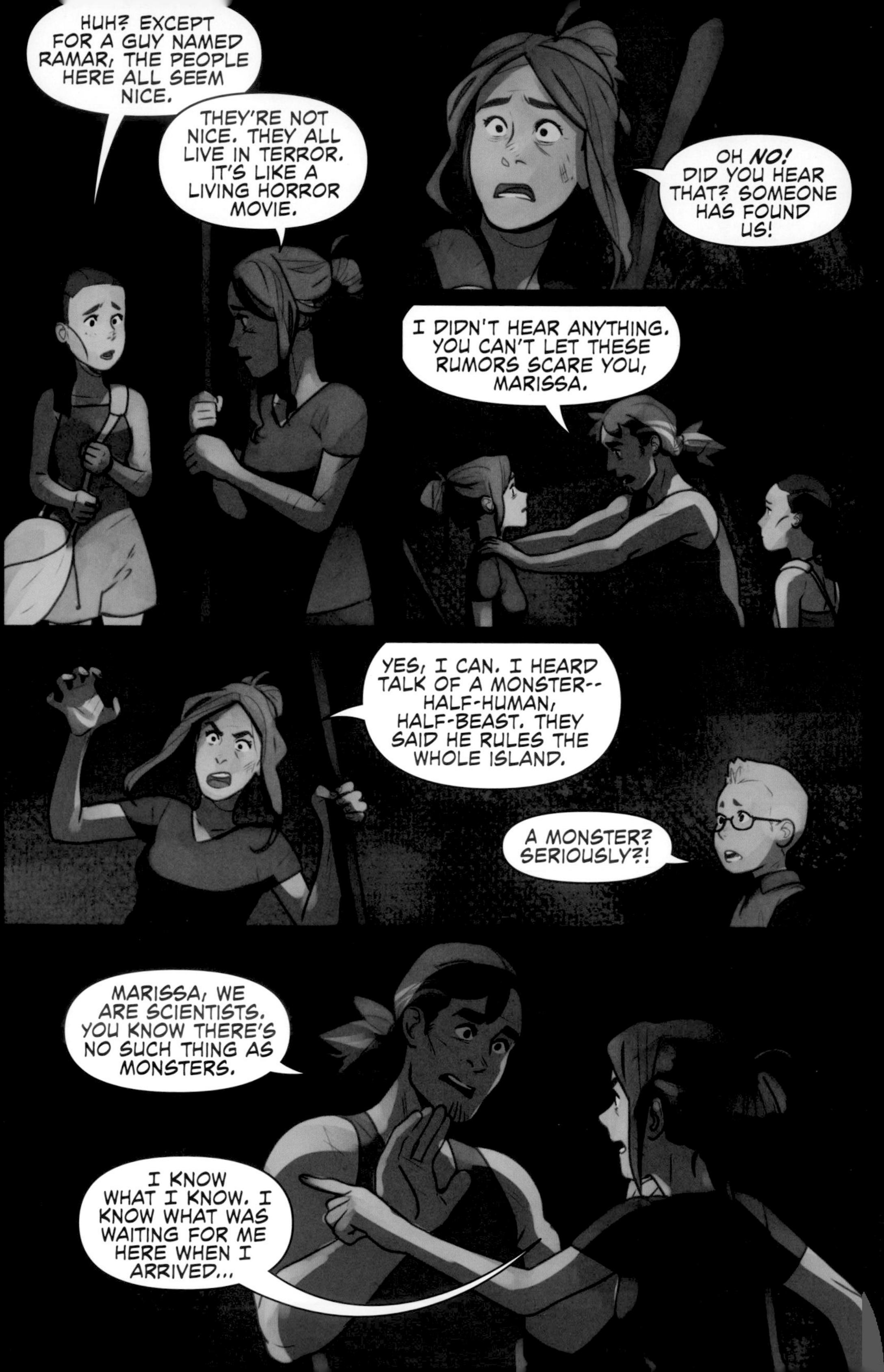

HUH? EXCEPT FOR A GUY NAMED RAMAR, THE PEOPLE HERE ALL SEEM NICE.
THEY'RE NOT NICE. THEY ALL LIVE IN TERROR. IT'S LIKE A LIVING HORROR MOVIE.
OH *NO!* DID YOU HEAR THAT? SOMEONE HAS FOUND US!
I DIDN'T HEAR ANYTHING. YOU CAN'T LET THESE RUMORS SCARE YOU, MARISSA.
YES, I CAN. I HEARD TALK OF A MONSTER--HALF-HUMAN, HALF-BEAST. THEY SAID HE RULES THE WHOLE ISLAND.
A MONSTER? SERIOUSLY?!
MARISSA, WE ARE SCIENTISTS. YOU KNOW THERE'S NO SUCH THING AS MONSTERS.
I KNOW WHAT I KNOW. I KNOW WHAT WAS WAITING FOR ME HERE WHEN I ARRIVED...

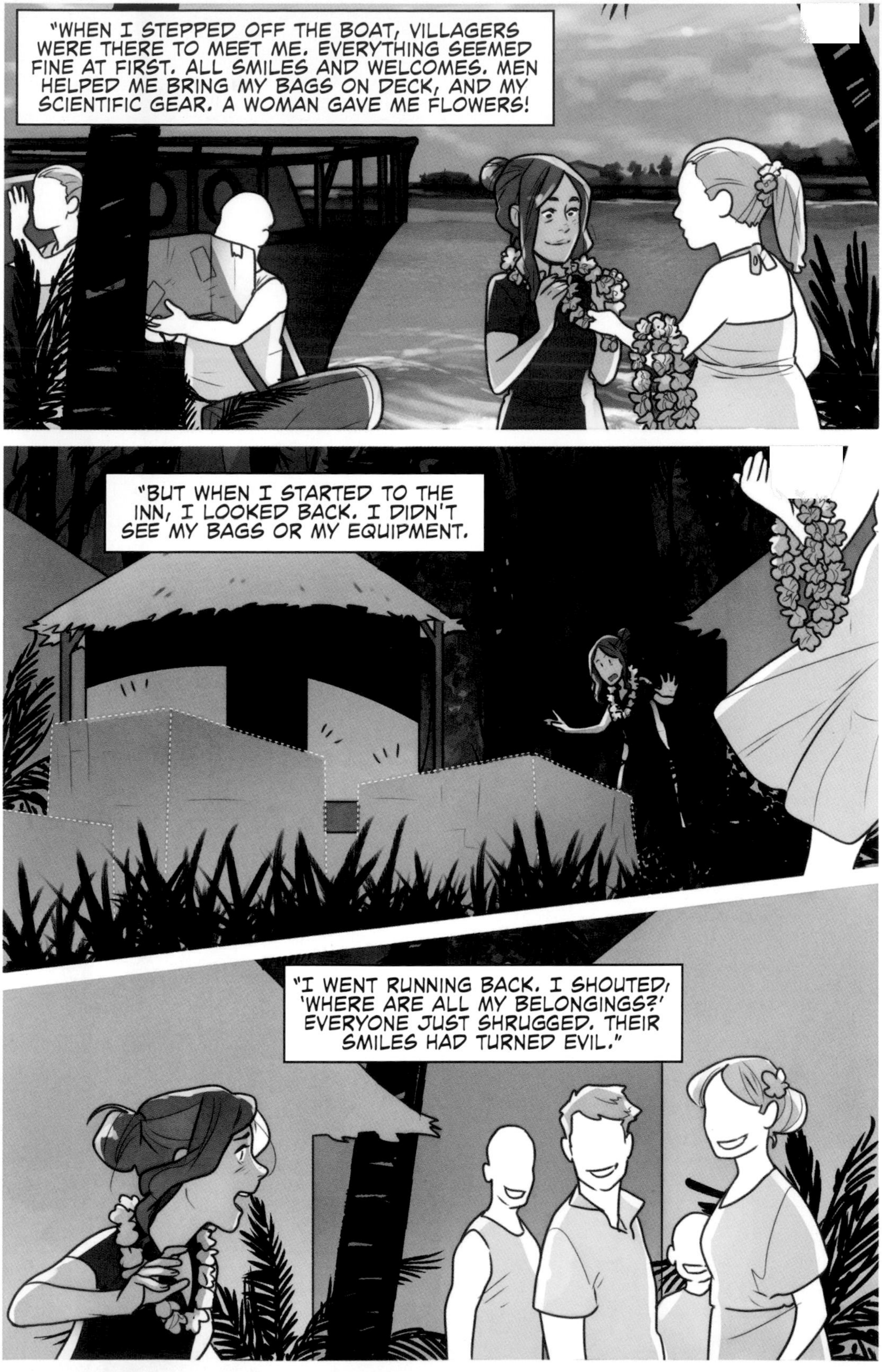
"WHEN I STEPPED OFF THE BOAT, VILLAGERS WERE THERE TO MEET ME. EVERYTHING SEEMED FINE AT FIRST. ALL SMILES AND WELCOMES. MEN HELPED ME BRING MY BAGS ON DECK, AND MY SCIENTIFIC GEAR. A WOMAN GAVE ME FLOWERS!
"BUT WHEN I STARTED TO THE INN, I LOOKED BACK. I DIDN'T SEE MY BAGS OR MY EQUIPMENT.
"I WENT RUNNING BACK. I SHOUTED, 'WHERE ARE ALL MY BELONGINGS?' EVERYONE JUST SHRUGGED. THEIR SMILES HAD TURNED EVIL."

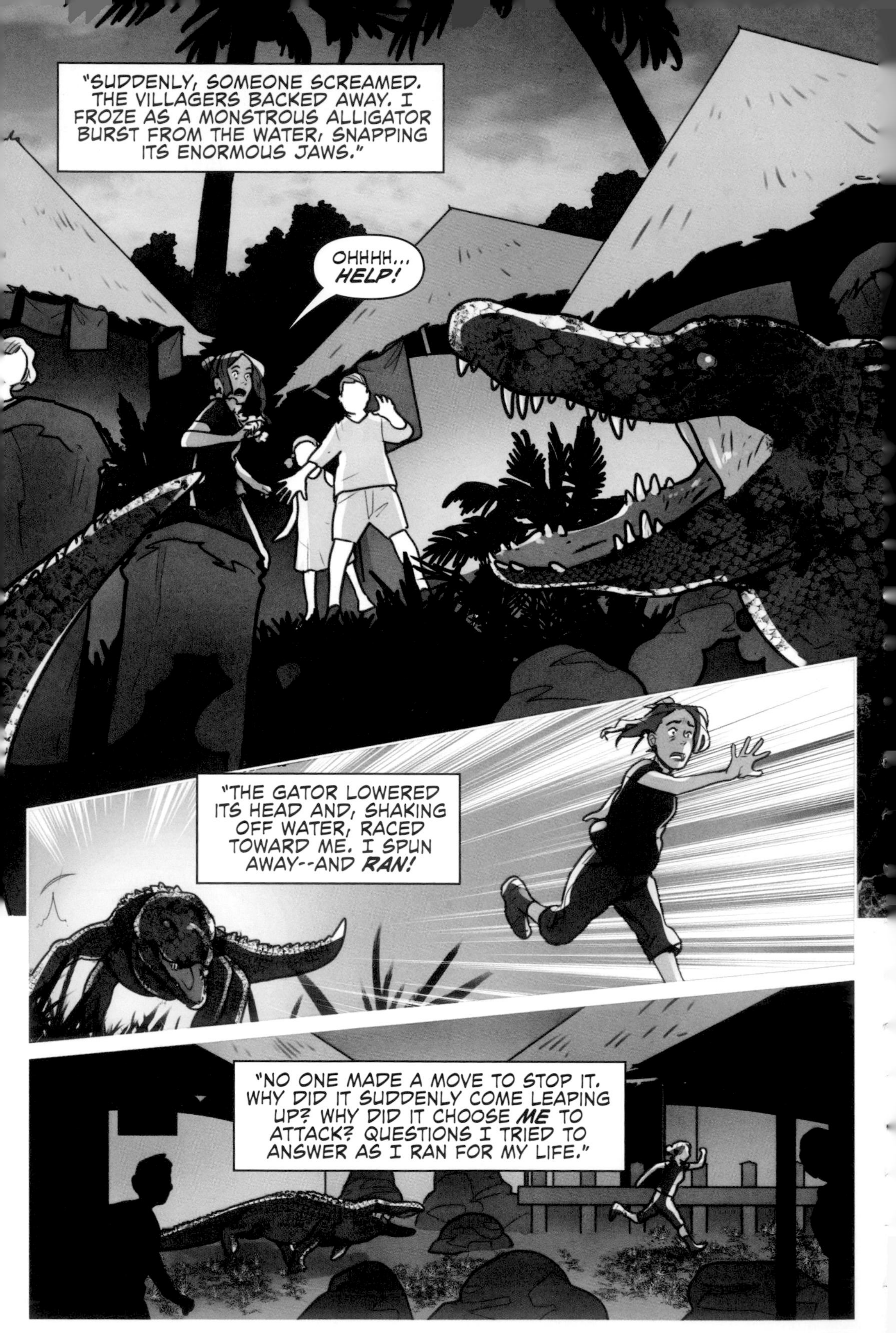
"SUDDENLY, SOMEONE SCREAMED. THE VILLAGERS BACKED AWAY. I FROZE AS A MONSTROUS ALLIGATOR BURST FROM THE WATER, SNAPPING ITS ENORMOUS JAWS."
OHHHH... *HELP!*
"THE GATOR LOWERED ITS HEAD AND, SHAKING OFF WATER, RACED TOWARD ME. I SPUN AWAY--AND *RAN!*
"NO ONE MADE A MOVE TO STOP IT. WHY DID IT SUDDENLY COME LEAPING UP? WHY DID IT CHOOSE *ME* TO ATTACK? QUESTIONS I TRIED TO ANSWER AS I RAN FOR MY LIFE."

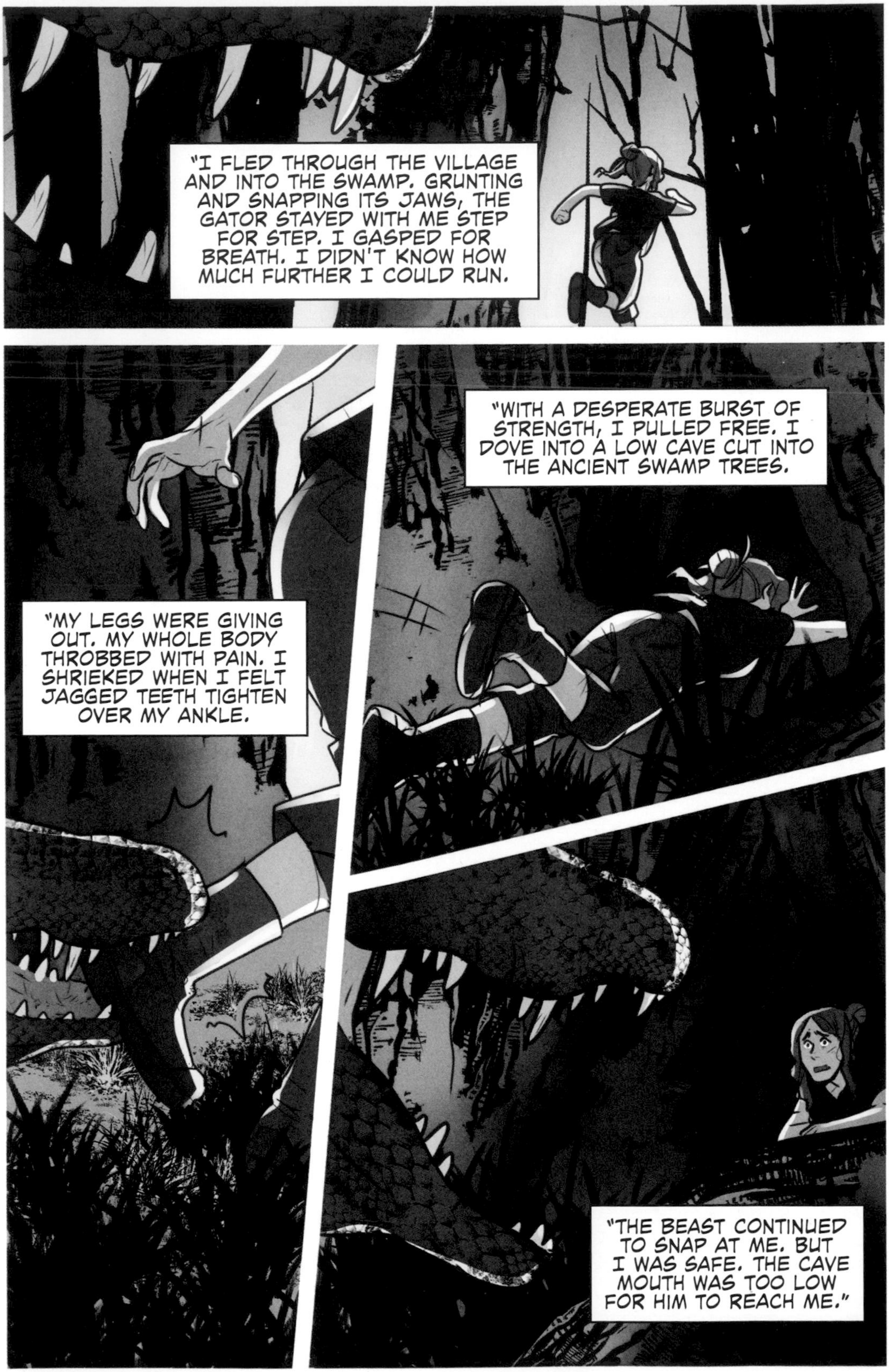
"I FLED THROUGH THE VILLAGE AND INTO THE SWAMP. GRUNTING AND SNAPPING ITS JAWS, THE GATOR STAYED WITH ME STEP FOR STEP. I GASPED FOR BREATH. I DIDN'T KNOW HOW MUCH FURTHER I COULD RUN.
"MY LEGS WERE GIVING OUT. MY WHOLE BODY THROBBED WITH PAIN. I SHRIEKED WHEN I FELT JAGGED TEETH TIGHTEN OVER MY ANKLE.
"WITH A DESPERATE BURST OF STRENGTH, I PULLED FREE. I DOVE INTO A LOW CAVE CUT INTO THE ANCIENT SWAMP TREES.
"THE BEAST CONTINUED TO SNAP AT ME. BUT I WAS SAFE. THE CAVE MOUTH WAS TOO LOW FOR HIM TO REACH ME."

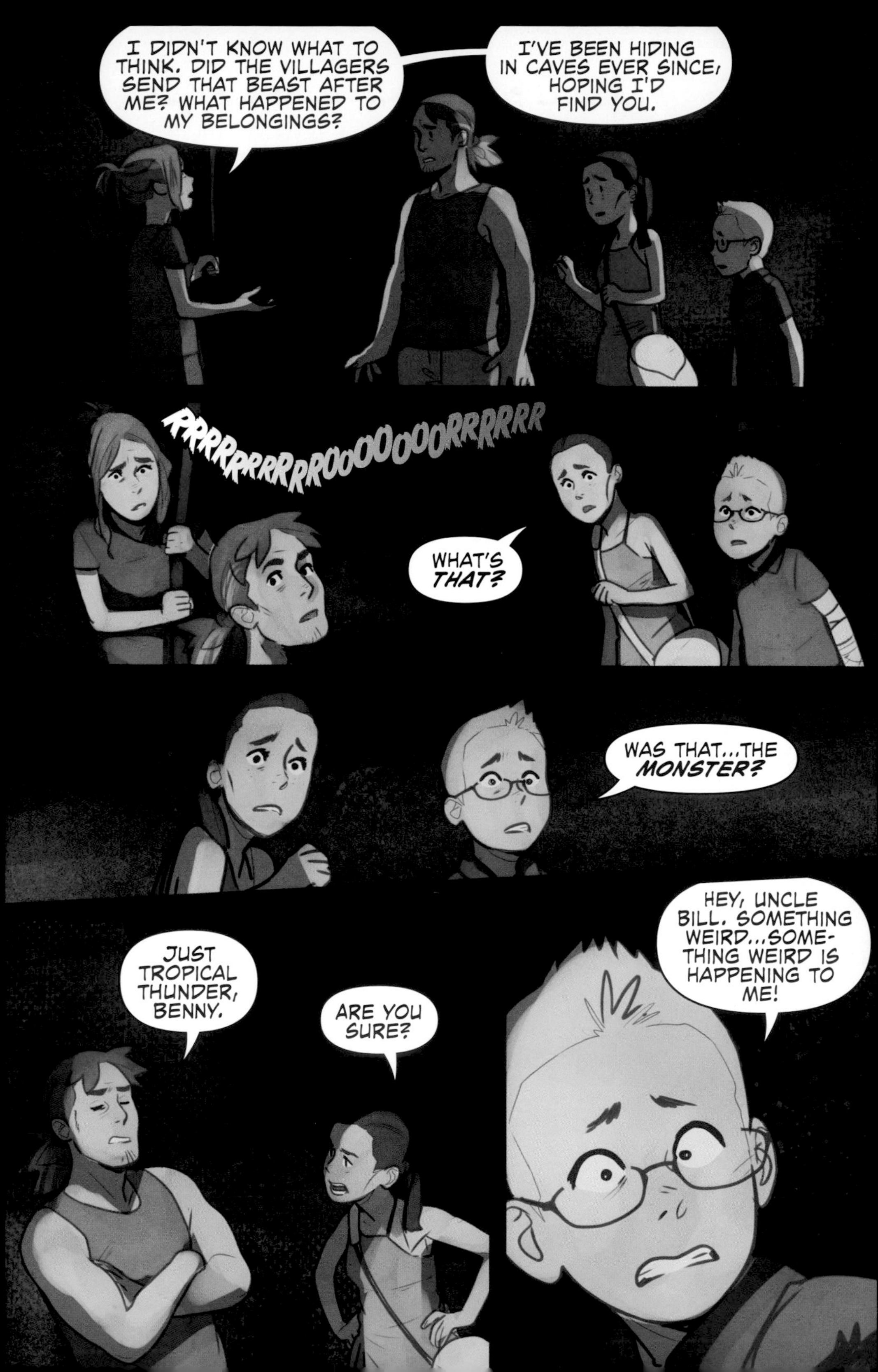
I DIDN'T KNOW WHAT TO THINK. DID THE VILLAGERS SEND THAT BEAST AFTER ME? WHAT HAPPENED TO MY BELONGINGS?
I'VE BEEN HIDING IN CAVES EVER SINCE, HOPING I'D FIND YOU.
RRRRRRRRRROOOOOOOORRRRRR
WHAT'S *THAT?*
WAS THAT...THE *MONSTER?*
JUST TROPICAL THUNDER, BENNY.
ARE YOU SURE?
HEY, UNCLE BILL. SOMETHING WEIRD...SOME-THING WEIRD IS HAPPENING TO ME!

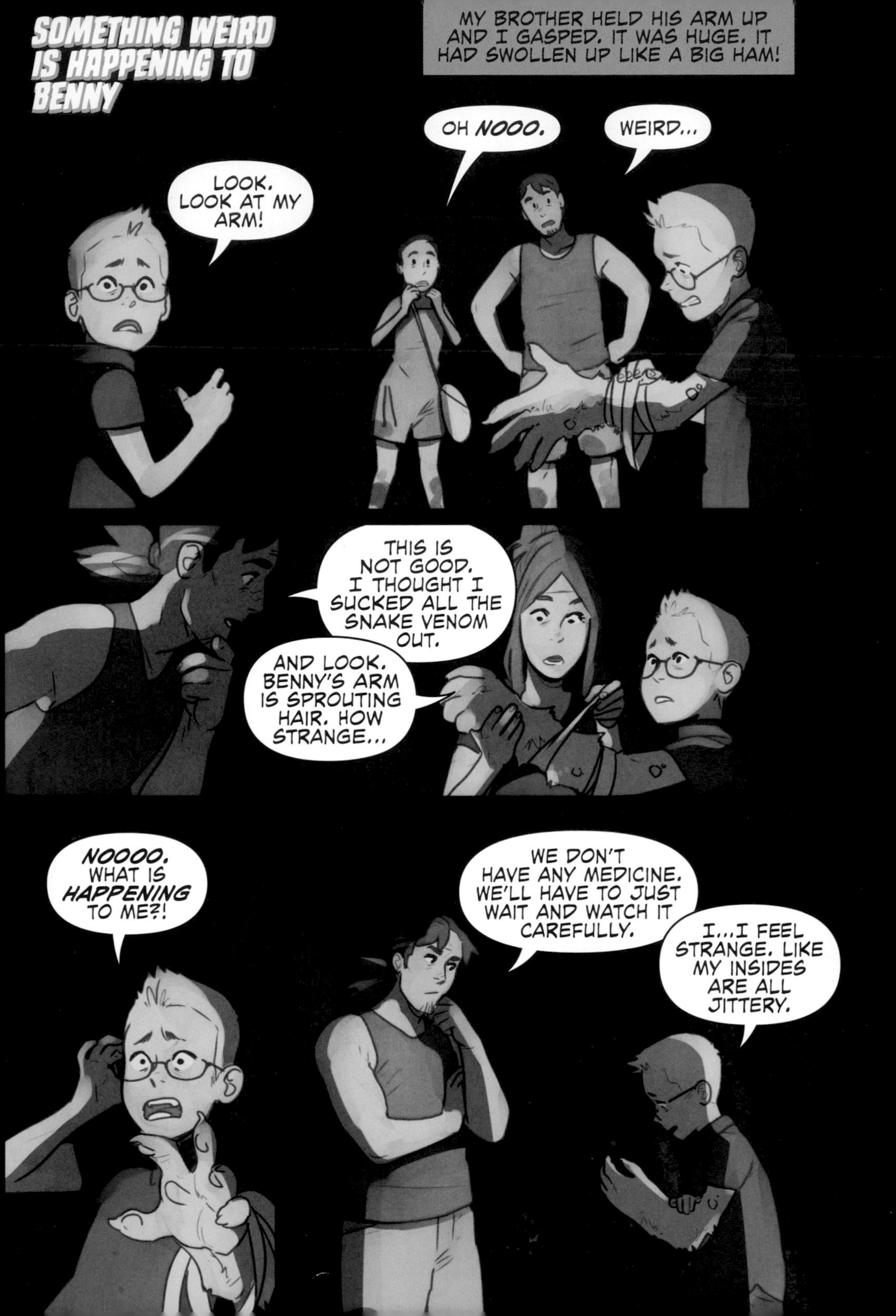
SOMETHING WEIRD IS HAPPENING TO BENNY
MY BROTHER HELD HIS ARM UP AND I GASPED. IT WAS HUGE. IT HAD SWOLLEN UP LIKE A BIG HAM!
LOOK. LOOK AT MY ARM!
OH NOOO.
WEIRD...
THIS IS NOT GOOD. I THOUGHT I SUCKED ALL THE SNAKE VENOM OUT.
AND LOOK. BENNY'S ARM IS SPROUTING HAIR. HOW STRANGE...
NOOOO. WHAT IS HAPPENING TO ME?!
WE DON'T HAVE ANY MEDICINE. WE'LL HAVE TO JUST WAIT AND WATCH IT CAREFULLY.
I...I FEEL STRANGE. LIKE MY INSIDES ARE ALL JITTERY.

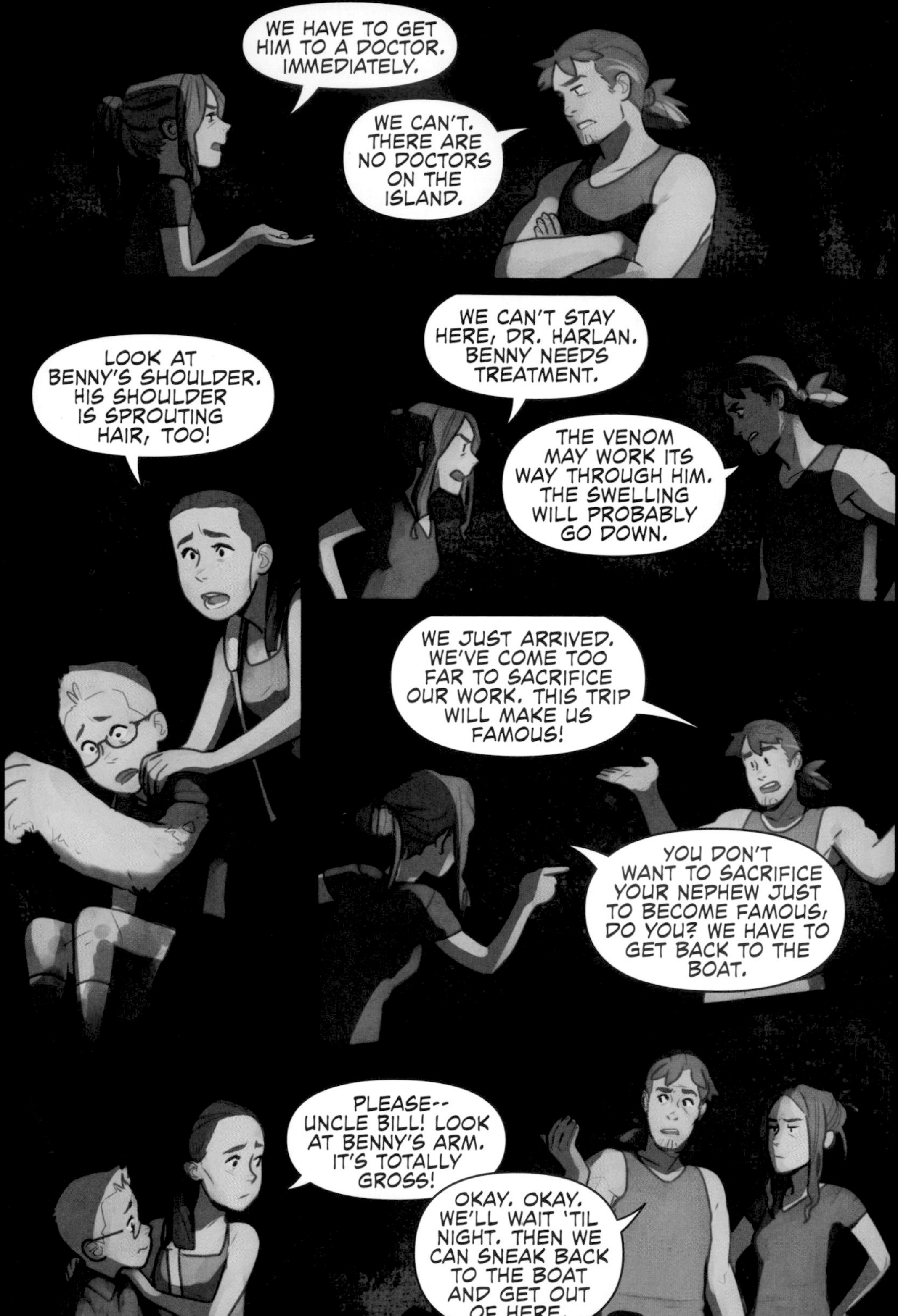
WE HAVE TO GET HIM TO A DOCTOR. IMMEDIATELY.
WE CAN'T. THERE ARE NO DOCTORS ON THE ISLAND.
LOOK AT BENNY'S SHOULDER. HIS SHOULDER IS SPROUTING HAIR, TOO!
WE CAN'T STAY HERE, DR. HARLAN. BENNY NEEDS TREATMENT.
THE VENOM MAY WORK ITS WAY THROUGH HIM. THE SWELLING WILL PROBABLY GO DOWN.
WE JUST ARRIVED. WE'VE COME TOO FAR TO SACRIFICE OUR WORK. THIS TRIP WILL MAKE US FAMOUS!
YOU DON'T WANT TO SACRIFICE YOUR NEPHEW JUST TO BECOME FAMOUS, DO YOU? WE HAVE TO GET BACK TO THE BOAT.
PLEASE-- UNCLE BILL! LOOK AT BENNY'S ARM. IT'S TOTALLY GROSS!
OKAY. OKAY. WE'LL WAIT 'TIL NIGHT. THEN WE CAN SNEAK BACK TO THE BOAT AND GET OUT OF HERE.

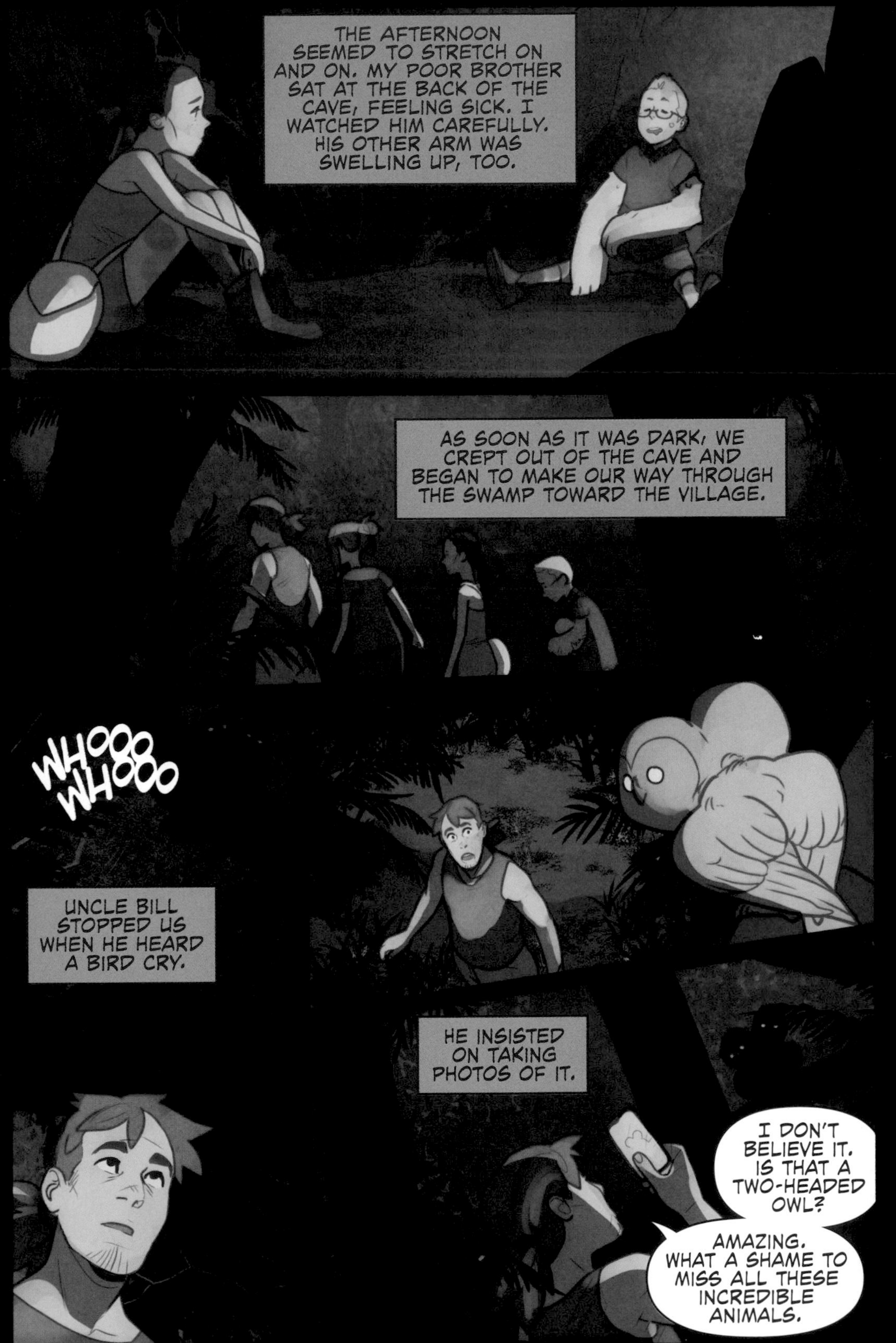
THE AFTERNOON SEEMED TO STRETCH ON AND ON. MY POOR BROTHER SAT AT THE BACK OF THE CAVE, FEELING SICK. I WATCHED HIM CAREFULLY. HIS OTHER ARM WAS SWELLING UP, TOO.
AS SOON AS IT WAS DARK, WE CREPT OUT OF THE CAVE AND BEGAN TO MAKE OUR WAY THROUGH THE SWAMP TOWARD THE VILLAGE.
WHOOO WHOOO
UNCLE BILL STOPPED US WHEN HE HEARD A BIRD CRY.
HE INSISTED ON TAKING PHOTOS OF IT.
I DON'T BELIEVE IT. IS THAT A TWO-HEADED OWL?
AMAZING. WHAT A SHAME TO MISS ALL THESE INCREDIBLE ANIMALS.

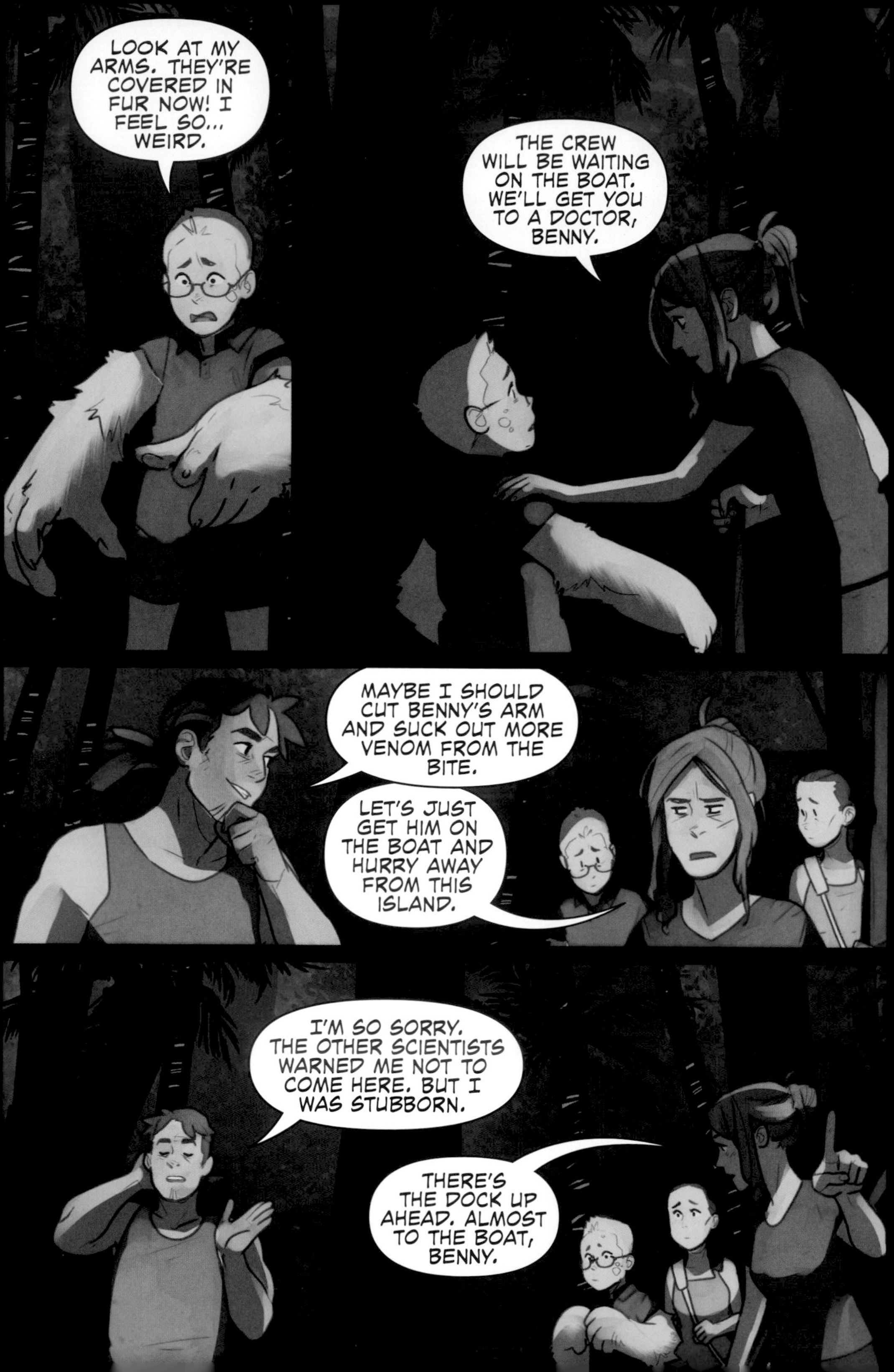
LOOK AT MY ARMS. THEY'RE COVERED IN FUR NOW! I FEEL SO... WEIRD.
THE CREW WILL BE WAITING ON THE BOAT. WE'LL GET YOU TO A DOCTOR, BENNY.
MAYBE I SHOULD CUT BENNY'S ARM AND SUCK OUT MORE VENOM FROM THE BITE.
LET'S JUST GET HIM ON THE BOAT AND HURRY AWAY FROM THIS ISLAND.
I'M SO SORRY. THE OTHER SCIENTISTS WARNED ME NOT TO COME HERE. BUT I WAS STUBBORN.
THERE'S THE DOCK UP AHEAD. ALMOST TO THE BOAT, BENNY.

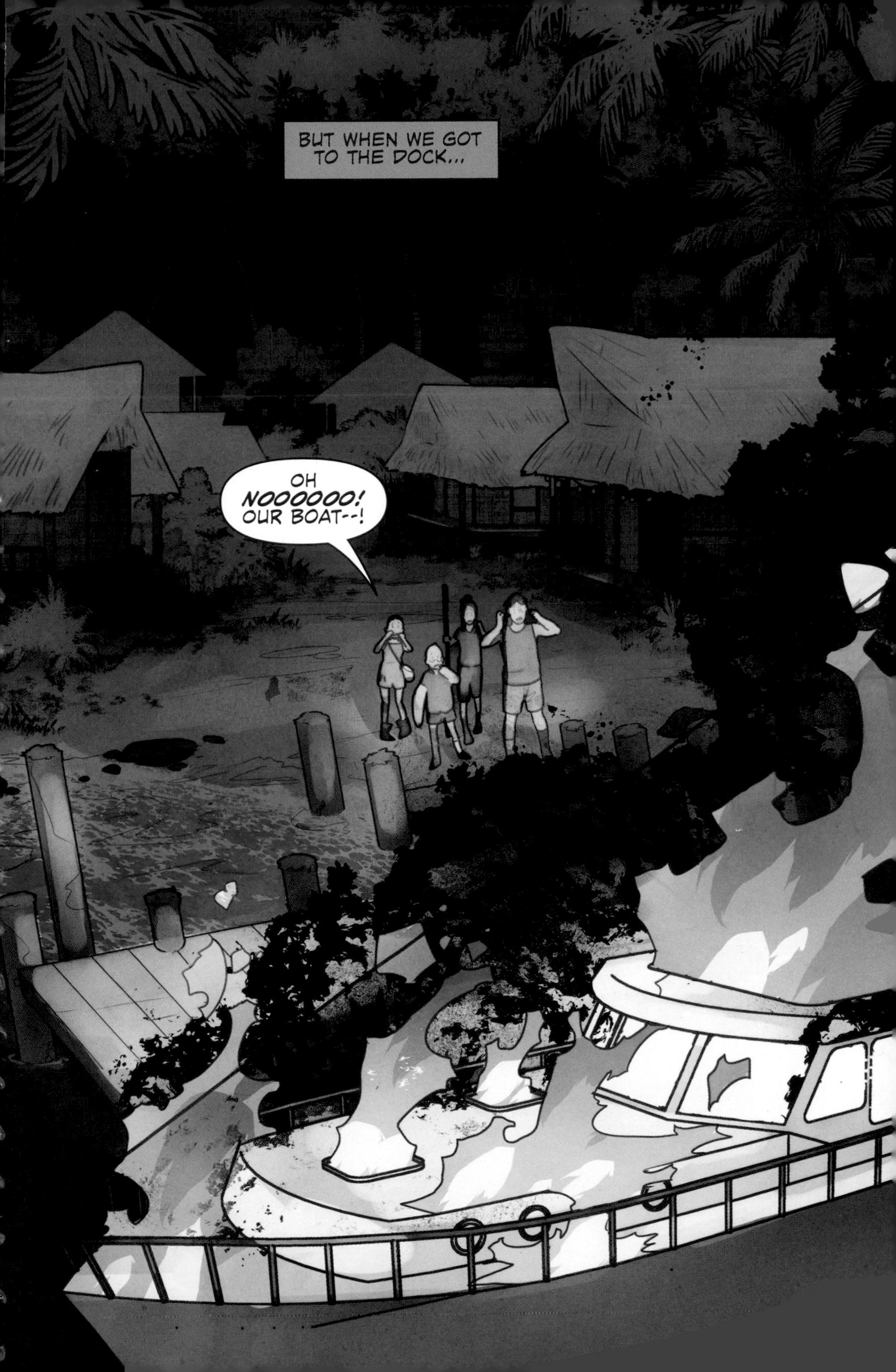
BUT WHEN WE GOT TO THE DOCK...
OH *NOOOOOO!* OUR BOAT--!

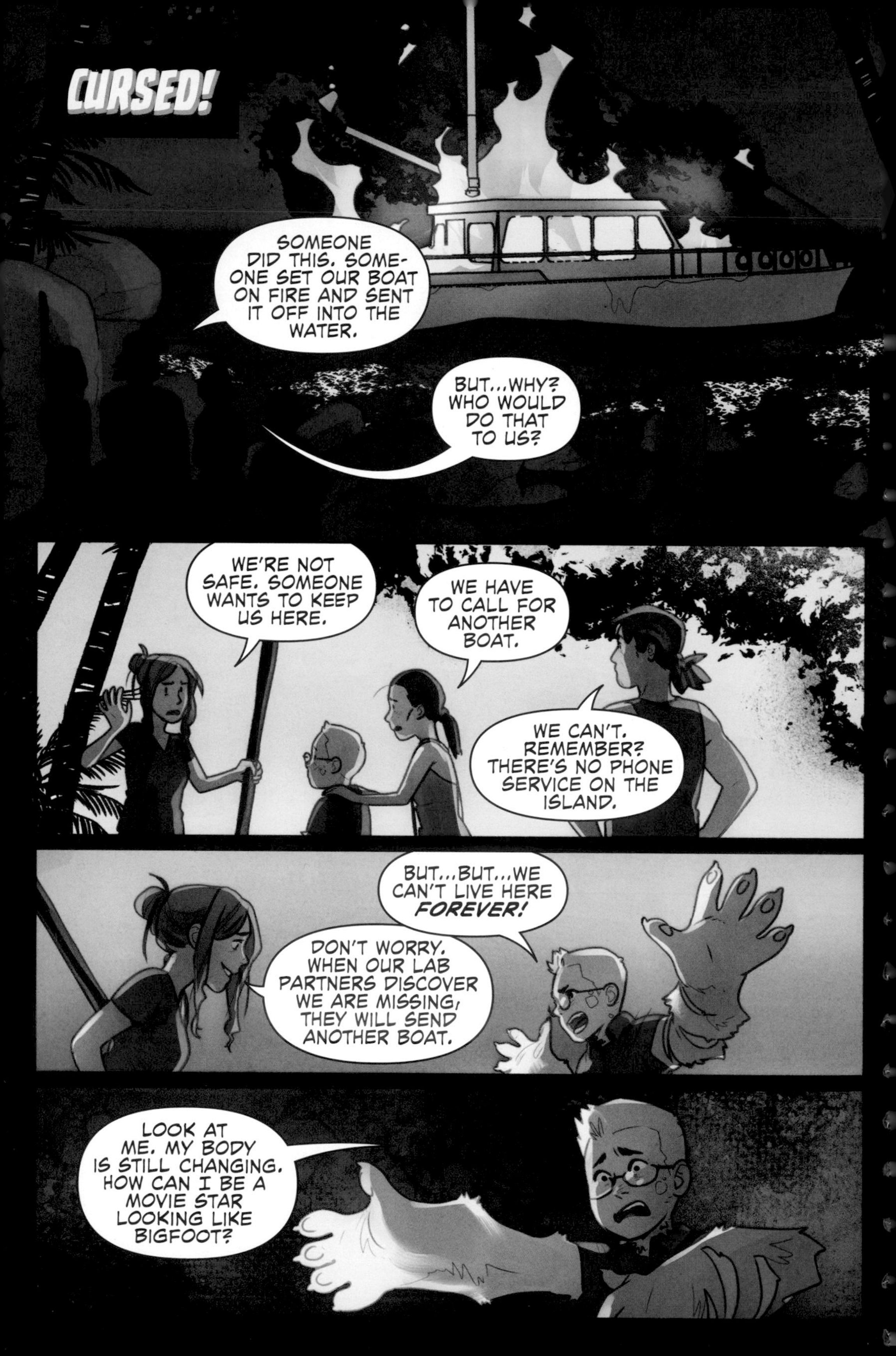
CURSED!
SOMEONE DID THIS. SOME-ONE SET OUR BOAT ON FIRE AND SENT IT OFF INTO THE WATER.
BUT...WHY? WHO WOULD DO THAT TO US?
WE'RE NOT SAFE. SOMEONE WANTS TO KEEP US HERE.
WE HAVE TO CALL FOR ANOTHER BOAT.
WE CAN'T. REMEMBER? THERE'S NO PHONE SERVICE ON THE ISLAND.
BUT...BUT...WE CAN'T LIVE HERE *FOREVER!*
DON'T WORRY. WHEN OUR LAB PARTNERS DISCOVER WE ARE MISSING, THEY WILL SEND ANOTHER BOAT.
LOOK AT ME. MY BODY IS STILL CHANGING. HOW CAN I BE A MOVIE STAR LOOKING LIKE BIGFOOT?

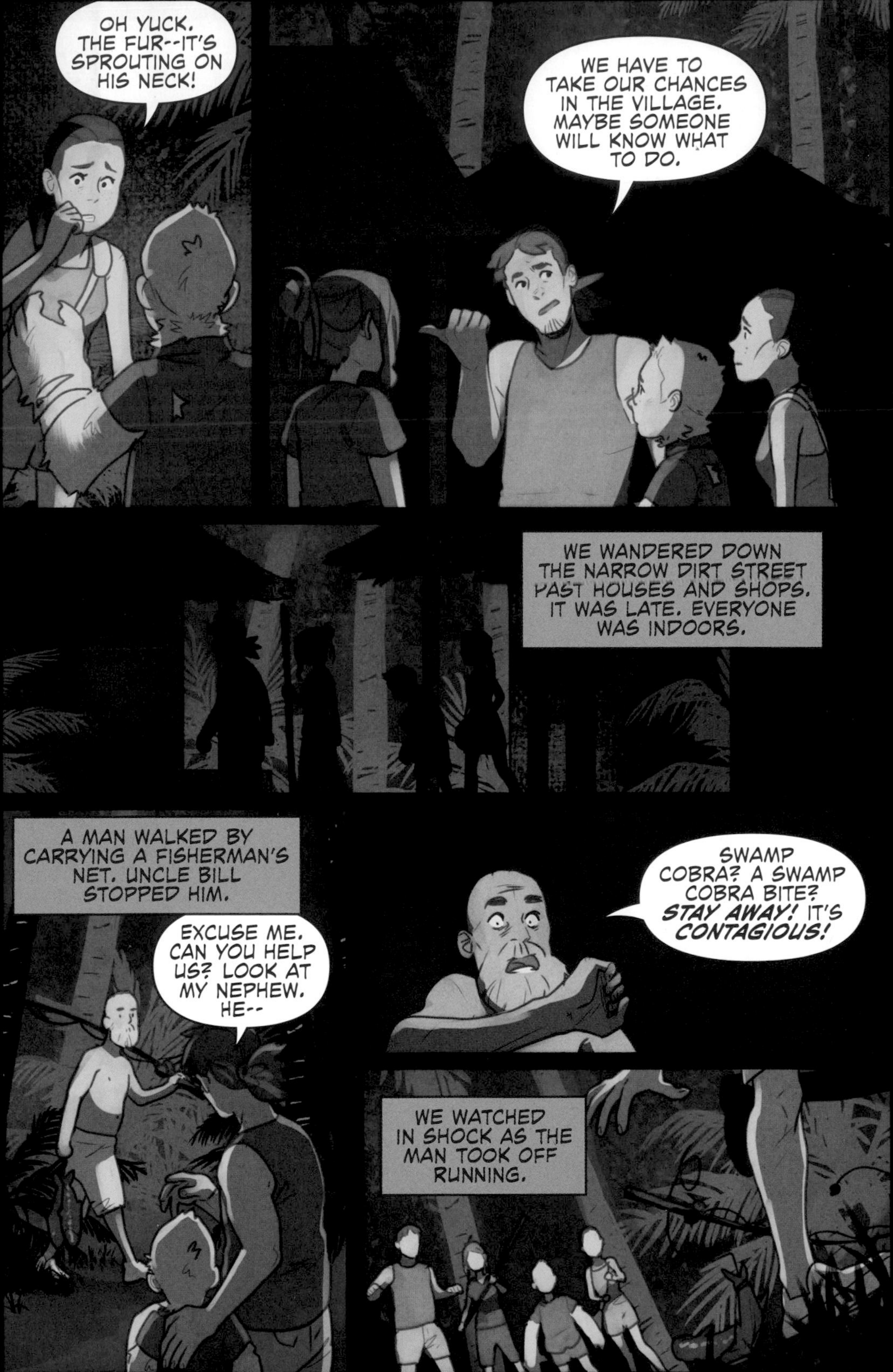
OH YUCK. THE FUR--IT'S SPROUTING ON HIS NECK!
WE HAVE TO TAKE OUR CHANCES IN THE VILLAGE. MAYBE SOMEONE WILL KNOW WHAT TO DO.
WE WANDERED DOWN THE NARROW DIRT STREET PAST HOUSES AND SHOPS. IT WAS LATE. EVERYONE WAS INDOORS.
A MAN WALKED BY CARRYING A FISHERMAN'S NET. UNCLE BILL STOPPED HIM.
EXCUSE ME. CAN YOU HELP US? LOOK AT MY NEPHEW. HE--
SWAMP COBRA? A SWAMP COBRA BITE? STAY AWAY! IT'S CONTAGIOUS!
WE WATCHED IN SHOCK AS THE MAN TOOK OFF RUNNING.

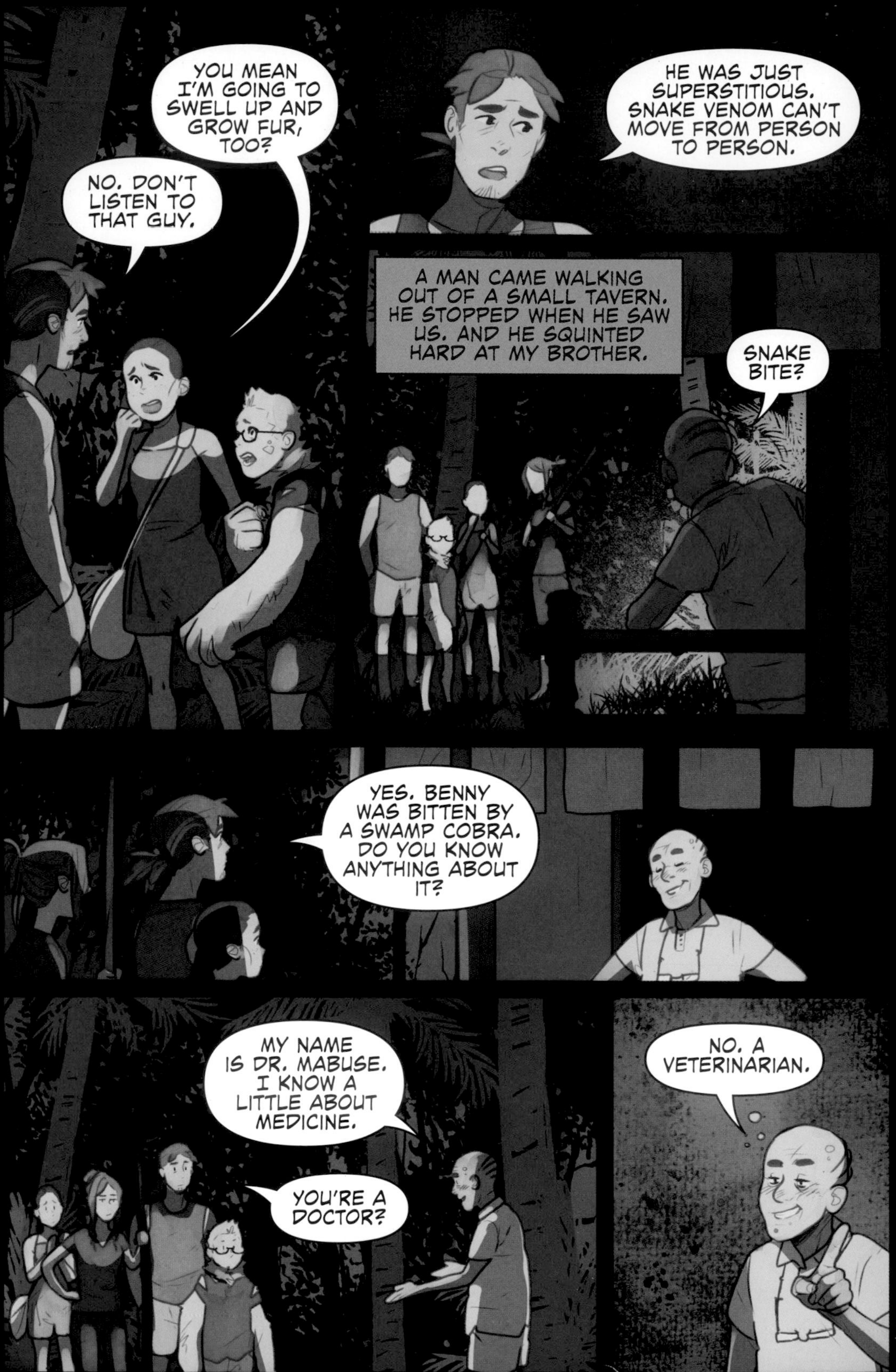

YOU MEAN I'M GOING TO SWELL UP AND GROW FUR, TOO?
NO. DON'T LISTEN TO THAT GUY.
HE WAS JUST SUPERSTITIOUS. SNAKE VENOM CAN'T MOVE FROM PERSON TO PERSON.
A MAN CAME WALKING OUT OF A SMALL TAVERN. HE STOPPED WHEN HE SAW US. AND HE SQUINTED HARD AT MY BROTHER.
SNAKE BITE?
YES. BENNY WAS BITTEN BY A SWAMP COBRA. DO YOU KNOW ANYTHING ABOUT IT?
MY NAME IS DR. MABUSE. I KNOW A LITTLE ABOUT MEDICINE.
YOU'RE A DOCTOR?
NO. A VETERINARIAN.